More Advance Praise

"Henderson combines a photojournalist's instinct for human drama with a trained academic's focus on nuance and precision to deliver a compelling debut that simultaneously informs and captivates. The book that I will be recommending to anyone looking to gain not just information, but true insight into the human impact of the complex and often conflicting realities of post-Cold War Europe."

— **Jonathan Liedl**, senior editor at *National Catholic Register*

"A well-researched and well-written series of accounts of life as an American service member in Europe. Henderson highlights the highs and sometimes tragic lows soldiers can find themselves in while living and working alongside their allies."

— **Joshua Skovlund**, staff writer at *Task & Purpose*

"Henderson's debut novel lives up to his reputation as a photographer. A must-read for young soldiers, veterans, and anyone else disillusioned with America's foreign policy."

— **Mark Granza**, founding editor of *IM-1776*

"*West from the Fallen Wall* skillfully weaves a tapestry of narratives that not only illuminates the geopolitical landscape but also humanizes the individuals behind the uniform, making this book an engaging and thought-provoking read, especially given today's Europe and the challenges it faces."

— **Martin Egnash**, former Marine reporter for *Stars and Stripes*

West from the Fallen Wall

Short Stories from the *Pax Americana* in Europe

Ryan Lucas Henderson

Introduction by Ben Braddock
Illustrations by Captain James Seawright, U.S. Army

SPADE & SCROLL

Spade & Scroll Press, LLC
queries@spadeandscroll.com
spadeandscroll.com

SPADE & SCROLL

Saint Paul, Minnesota

©2024 by Ryan Lucas Henderson
You can follow Ryan by searching @ryanlucasphoto on Instagram and X.

This is one of one thousand books in the first printing of the first edition of this title.

All rights to the content of this book are reserved. There are no parts that may be reproduced without permission from Spade & Scroll Press.

This book was printed in the United States of America and set in Baskerville font. The cover was designed by Geoffrey Krawczyk. The introduction was written by Ben Braddock. The illustrations were drawn by Captain James Seawright. The book was edited by Lucas Menzies. The author photo was taken by Giorgia Greselin.

The translations of Ezekiel 37:11 and 37:12-14 are by Lucas Menzies, based on the Hebrew text presented in the *Biblia Hebraica Stuttgartensia*.

Advanced praise blurbs are credited exclusively to the writers themselves, not the outlets or organizations to which they belong. The reviews represent the opinions of their writers, not the mentioned outlets, organizations, or companies.

The content of this book is entirely fiction. Though it reflects reality, the characters, settings, and events are fictitious. Any resemblance to real people is a coincidence and completely unintentional.

Library of Congress Control Number: 2024933780
ISBN: 9798990072206

Table of Contents

Introduction by Ben Braddock vii
1) Rockets' Red Glare 1
2) The Schnitzel and the Shark 15
3) Red Sheepskin 41
4) Pavlo's Horror 73
5) As the Romans 81
6) When We're Away 133
7) Nobody Passes Here 165
8) Go the Spoils 181
9) Forest of Dry Bones 203
Acknowledgements 254
Works Referenced 255

Introduction

Peace, and the absence of war. These are two entirely different things. What we called peace in Europe during that period that lay roughly between Kosovo and the Russian invasion of Ukraine was not marked by feelings of tranquility, harmony, and security, but by the feeling of being watched by some unknown creature lurking in the brush. I had this feeling while hunting in the High Sierra backcountry and over the course of several days became increasingly convinced that I was being stalked by some malevolent cryptid. I never got a clear look at whatever it was, only flashes of movement out of the corner of my eye, the sound of a branch snapping, a whiff of strange odor that set the hair on the back of my neck to sticking up. It was much more nerve-wracking than facing a clear danger. I have come face to face with several grizzlies in the Rockies while unarmed, and none of those encounters gave me a dread like the thing I never actually encountered.

It is strange that such a terrible thing as war can feel like a relief once it is actually under way. The build-up to war is what is intolerable, a building, tormenting tension and the constantly repeated and never answered question of what will actually happen, or if anything will happen at all. The tension finally reaches the breaking point. The rubber band snaps. The tank engines start. The planes head for their targets. Energy is now being directed into activity. The long-delayed but always expected conflict has finally arrived.

This book deals with the before-time, before the coronavirus, before the Russian invasion of Ukraine. That strange time in modern Europe when it felt as if the end of history had actually been achieved. There were no longer any apparent threats from state actors as there had been in the Cold War days. By all accounts the Russian and European economies were too interwoven and codependent for the relationship to ever fully sour again. The threats were confined to the shadows. NATO continued training for confrontation with an undefined enemy that, it was assumed, would take the form of a peer military power using conventional weapons and rules of warfare, but Europe's actual security threat had evolved.

I remember returning with a group of friends to the base housing in Vicenza one foggy November night and being greeted at the gate by freaked-out MPs yelling and pointing their rifles at us. While we had been at the circus on the edge of town, watching bears ride bicycles around a ring, Islamist terrorists had launched a wave of mass shootings and suicide bombings in Paris. In such moments, the threat felt intense and defined. These moments were few and far between. Mostly there was just an uncomfortable undercurrent of *something*. America's security umbrella still hung over Europeans' heads, even as the sun had been shining for years. But when bad weather did flare up, the umbrella was of no use. In fact, it usually functioned as a lightning rod. In those years there were frequent reminders that America's empire had worn out its welcome in some quarters. Reminders that were delivered with varying degrees of subtlety. The stories within *West from the Fallen Wall* depict with piercing poignance this relationship between Americans and Europeans and the subtle complications and dramas that are an invisible feature of life in a peacetime military alliance.

The stories in this book touch on so many aspects of the American experience in Europe. There are the cultural frictions, the resentments, the inane foibles of military bureaucracy, and old sore spots; but there are also the moments of mutual affinity, respect, and affection. Europe is the place from where so many Americans derive their ancestry. Our forebears may have left to cross the ocean a long time ago, but there is something about the place that still resonates in the marrow, and something about the people that stirs faint memories.

The closing story, "Forest of Dry Bones," is a true pièce de résistance. I will not give any of the stories away with summaries because they are layered and arranged in such a way that you must allow them to breathe and draw you into experiencing them sequentially, as a series of vignettes that will form a complete painting only when you've read the last line. But I will say that the theme of that closing story recalls to mind a visit I once paid to the American military cemetery at Draguignan. I struck up a conversation with a groundskeeper there after I stopped to compliment the immaculate landscaping. He told me that the people of the town consider it a great honor to look after the graves of the Americans who died in the liberation of France. The French conception of honor carries with it an active sense of ongoing purpose. Eight decades on from liberation and Le Souvenir Franco-Americain, an active society of local citizens, still carries on the special tradition of honoring the Americans each Memorial Day and on other military holidays throughout the year. The society also pays the way for two American relatives of the dead to visit the cemetery each year and be hosted and honored by the members of the society. There are fewer and fewer known, remaining relatives to invite. The members of the society are growing older as well, with less interest from younger generations now than in the past and fewer funds available to carry on the activities. But they carry on.

I recently visited my great-uncle, the last surviving veteran of World War II in my family. He will soon be 101 years old. He fought in the Battle of the Bulge and spent the end of the war in a POW camp. I grew up listening in rapt interest to him, my grandfather, and other veterans when they would talk about the war. A few years ago in Baden-Württemberg, a German friend took me to visit his grandmother, and she talked about her memories as a little girl in Germany before and during the war, showing off a scar left by shrapnel from an American bomb and a picture of her American husband she met in the 60s. She passed away in the first winter of coronavirus. There are precious few left who remember the war firsthand, and before much longer there will be none at all. Much of the American-European relationship has been built on mutual connections to the war, and as those connections fade away with time, either something will replace them, or the relationship will change. And when my generation grows old and passes away, the memories of *Pax Americana* in Europe will pass away too.

But at least there will be this book.

— Ben Braddock, January 2024

For Giorgia, whom I met in the midst of all this.

"NATO's first mission is now nearly complete. But if we are to fulfill our vision — our European vision — the challenges of the next 40 years will ask no less of us."

— President George H. W. Bush, May 31st, 1989

The following stories take place in Europe during the post-Cold War era, in the years preceding the coronavirus pandemic.

They were written from the Italian and American lockdowns, prior to the Russian invasion of Ukraine.

Rockets' Red Glare

It was still dark when First Lieutenant Kovač walked briskly across the driveway toward his car. The small bed-and-breakfast where he'd been staying the past two weeks sat quietly under the looming eyes of a high plateau in central Croatia. Its dark silhouette cast a shadow between the moonlight and the now blackened pastures and vineyards that defined the property. The spirit in Kovač's step betrayed a fragile hope he had not felt in years, one he couldn't help but give into. His heart beat faster as he sat in his car and slammed shut the door. He paused for a moment to breathe in the fresh, cold air and then slowly pushed it out, his breath filling the dashboard.

Forward, he thought, as he started his car and began his morning drive to a rural and rarely used military training ground on the border of the city of Petrinja.

"You were chosen for this mission," he whispered to himself as his car limped down the road. "The Croatian Armed Forces depends on you. It's a very political job."

He nodded, catching a glimpse of himself in the rearview mirror, and then looked away. Embarrassingly old for a first lieutenant, his less-than-remarkable career had been spent caught between the shadow of his father's courageous military accomplishments forged during the birth of the young country and the crushing bureaucracies of a militia transforming into a professional army. He was heading toward obscurity, and he knew it all too well.

A small sign quickly came into view as Kovač swallowed a nervous lump in his throat.

"Petrinja," he said. "One more day…. One more day and then… what?"

His thoughts raced.

Coming to a stop sign, he reached into the passenger seat and pulled a packet of papers from a leather binder. Examining the contents as he drove, he flipped to the middle of the packet and ran his finger down the page until it rested on the day's date, the last line on the page. A single acronym sat beside it: LFX.

"And with you," he said through a broken voice, "I will start a turning point in my career."

He threw the papers back on the seat beside him.

Turning onto an unpaved frontage road just outside the city, Kovač pushed his glasses up his long nose, where they rested for a moment, only to slide down once more as the car bounced along the path that led up a hill and past a pasture full of grazing sheep. The road was choppy, and Kovač had to be attentive to avoid the fissures in the road that had been filled in by water from heavy rains the day before.

"I might have accomplished the impossible," he said as a meager smile formed on his parted lips.

Wiping his mouth and clearing his throat, he dropped the car into third gear and sped up the hill, winding past stacks of neatly chopped wood and shaggy dogs and quaint, stone houses that came all the way to the road. It was a cold morning in autumn, and smoke drifted from the chimneys of those roadside houses, inside of which children were forced by their parents to remain whenever the military came to town to use the training ground.

"You are too kind, my dear American friend, too kind," he said to himself giddily as his heart beat slightly faster and his smile widened across his face.

"The honor, I assure you, is all mine," Kovač exclaimed as he simulated a handshake with the air above the shift knobs.

"I wonder," he continued, "if I may have a few of your Meals-Ready-To-Eat? My son is always watching American army movies, and, you know, we don't really have these here. Why, thank you, sir! I know he will be so excited. You are too kind!"

Kovač's smile erupted into a joyous laughter that filled the car as he careened down a straight-away beneath arches of twisting, barren branches.

"You want to recommend me to your embassy?" he asked as he placed his hand over his heart.

"Yes! Yes! I think the support battalion can spare me for now. If I am needed at the U.S. Embassy, of course they will understand!"

Visions of his future flashed before his eyes: respect at work, respect at home, and, most of all, living up to the high expectations inherited through his surname.

He raised his hands above his greasy, curly hair and snapped his fingers to the rhythm of a Croatian folk song.

The road turned to even rougher gravel as the sun finally broke over the last of the tall trees and exposed in harsh, morning sunlight rows of uniformly spaced sleeping tents on one side of the dirt path and a compound of poorly built facilities of concrete and unpainted metal opposing them. All this sat on the far side of a run-down military checkpoint that Kovač slowly approached while he opened his window, his documents already prepared for inspection.

"What's your business here, mister?" an American private shouted at the car as he tossed his cigarette onto the ground and stomped it out.

The young American bore an attitude of brazen suspicion of Kovač, who shifted his wide-eyed, searching gaze to the second guard, a skinny, Croatian soldier waiting for his turn to speak up.

"Okay. Everyday - he - here," the Croatian guard said in broken English as he pointed to the car.

He was disregarded by the young American.

"Well, I'm still gonna need to see some papers."

"Yes, of course. Here you go, sir."

"And what did you say your business here was, mister?" the American asked as he gazed confusedly at the documents.

"I am the liaison between your army and mine, as well as the city of Petrinja," Kovač said with a smile.

"Ask him," he continued as he gestured toward the skinny, Croatian guard. "He sees me come in every day."

The American ignored the request.

"Well, I haven't heard anything about this. I'm gonna have to call my sergeant," he said, handing the documents back to Kovač. "Don't go anywhere, mister."

The young American stepped away from the car as Kovač exchanged annoyed glances with the skinny Croatian.

"Hello, staff sergeant. It's Brady," the American said over the two-way radio.

There was no response.

"Staff sergeant, it's Brady."

All three exchanged looks as the American grew visibly nervous.

A moment later, a monotone voice came over the radio.

"What is it, Brady?"

"I've got a person here saying he's some kind of lee-ayson, staff sergeant. Should I let him in?"

"A what, Brady?"

"A lee-ays-on, staff sergeant."

Kovač spoke up, telling the young American to give the sergeant his name, but was greeted with a pointer finger in the air and the direction of, "Hold on, now."

The voice came back over the radio.

"Is he military, Brady?"

"He's wearing a uniform, staff sergeant."

"Is he Croatian?"

The young American looked toward the skinny Croatian, studying his uniform in detail, then turned his stare to Kovač, squinting.

"Yeah, I think he is, staff sergeant. Uniform looks Croatian."

"I'll be right down. Don't let him go anywhere, Brady. It's the last day of the exercise, and we're in the middle of the LFX. Live rounds are about to start flying downrange. Wouldn't want this guy to catch a stray bullet."

Kovač's ears perked up as he heard the sergeant's response.

"The live-fire exercise has already begun?" he asked the American impatiently.

He received another finger of instruction to wait his turn, along with a harsh look of reprimand.

"Roger that, staff sergeant," the American said as he strutted back toward Kovač.

"Alright, mister, I can't let you past this checkpoint. They're already shootin' live downrange, and you're gonna need a guide to the tactical operations center."

Hearing they had already begun, Kovač cursed under his breath in his native language and threw his car into gear.

Breaking through the checkpoint's gate, hastily constructed of PVC pipe and wood, Kovač left in a cloud of dust the American, who, having been thoroughly caught off guard, immediately got back on the radio and told his sergeant, "The Croatian is past the gate! He's going for the TOC!"

The skinny, Croatian guard laughed.

Knowing where the tactical operations center was, as he'd been working at the site for the past two weeks, Kovač sped into the dirt parking lot between two of the drafty, metal buildings within a compound overlooking a large valley below. Taking several deep breaths before walking in the door, he tried to slow his heartbeat and calm his nerves. He knew the staff sergeant wouldn't be far behind.

"Good morning, gentlemen," he said as he entered the room, finding Major Meyers, the head of a U.S. task force from the diplomatic mission to NATO and the man currently overseeing the exercise during a tour of various training grounds across the European theater.

"Ah, I believe we've located our intruder, gentlemen!" Major Meyers said as he put down his binoculars and turned to smile at Kovač from the large, glass window on the far side of the room. "A little late, though, aren't you, Kovač? We heard you had to barge through the gate just to get here! Were you stuck in rush hour traffic? I know these roads can get pretty busy with sheep this time of day."

The major exchanged looks with one of the first sergeants on his staff, a crusty, old man, who grimaced back, not at all amused that the major was making light of Kovač's breach onto the training ground.

Kovač offered nervous laughter, and he crossed the room.

"Late, sir? I thought the LFX was not scheduled to begin until 7:00 a.m.?"

"0700? Hell, no. This is a live-fire. Need to start early if we're going to get all the platoons through the lane. Here, take these," he said as he handed Kovač the binoculars and slapped him on the back, pushing him forward one step.

Kovač was a heavy man, but the major was tall and strong and younger than him.

"Thank you, sir," he said, raising the binoculars to his eyes.

"You're just in time to watch second platoon make their way through the lane. You're gonna love this."

"And everything is still as we discussed, sir? Nothing was added to the itinerary?"

"There might be a surprise or two," said the dark-haired Major Meyers with a mischievous smile.

"What do you mean, sir?"

Before the major could answer, an out-of-breath staff sergeant barged through the door and locked eyes with Kovač. Throwing his arms in the air, he shouted, "What the fuck do you think you're doing?!" and crossed the room in three quick strides.

"That's quite enough, staff sergeant!" said the major in a voice raised above the commotion of the room.

The staff sergeant stopped in his tracks, stupefied, his mouth agape.

"That's an officer you're talking to, staff sergeant," Major Meyers continued.

8

"But, sir, he broke through the front gate," replied the staff sergeant impetuously.

"And you, staff sergeant, have lost your military bearing."

Irritated, the major turned back to the window that overlooked the valley below. Second platoon was in position to begin their attack. With Kovač watching, the staff sergeant exhaled and turned around, looking in disbelief at the first sergeant, his immediate boss, while two of the lieutenants on the major's staff stood quietly on the side of the room. Without speaking, the crusty first sergeant gestured toward the door, which swung in the autumn wind. The staff sergeant exhaled again, straightened his back, and left through the door he'd just barged through.

The room remained silent for a few moments until the major, looking at the binoculars, spouted, "Well, if you're not going to use them, I will."

He took the binoculars from a pensive Kovač, who was trying to come up with an easy and polite way to ask what surprises the major was referring to.

Gazing through the binoculars, the major saw that second platoon had begun their attack. Two squads were in the process of rushing through the woods on the eastern side of the valley, just below the observation post, while two other squads navigated their way through a maze of ravines and trenches bordering the southern edge of the area. Converging in a pincer movement, the four squads descended on their objective, which lied on the clearing in the valley. The major lowered the binoculars.

"I can feel you burning a hole in my head with that stare of yours, first sergeant," said Major Meyers. "Anything you'd like to add to the conversation?"

"No, sir. Nothing to add," the crusty first sergeant responded through gritted, yellow teeth.

Major Meyers turned around to face the first sergeant.

"He's a Croatian, for fuck's sake," he said to his subordinate, raising his eyebrows. "This is a *Croatian* military training ground."

"Yes, sir. No questions from me, sir," replied the first sergeant.

"And besides," continued Major Meyers as a smile returned to his face, "we *are* guests here."

He turned back to Kovač.

"Isn't that right, Kovač?" he said, slapping him on the back once more.

Looking up at Major Meyers timidly, Kovač, who had been deep in thought and only passively paying attention to the conversation, asked through a cracking voice, "Sir, what surprises do you have planned for the live-fire?"

"What kind of a surprise would it be if I told you, Kovač?"

Kovač cleared his throat.

"Sir, you do know why I'm here, don't you?"

"Of course, to ensure we don't blow up the Petrinj-ites," replied the major in jest, looking back at the two lieutenants on the side of the room and casually passing them a wink. "Don't worry, Kovač. Nothing is going to happen. You're looking at the most advanced military in the world. I think our anti-tank rockets can find their targets."

"Anti-tank, sir? Please do not tell me you're firing live AT-4 rockets. It's not about stray rockets; we're in a valley, and there's nothing to hit.... It's about the noise!"

"Kovač, why do you think we're out here?" the major spat back.

"Sir, with all due respect, I told you exactly what you are and aren't allowed to do at this training ground. You've already had soldiers firing after 9:00 p.m. on weeknights. Thank God no one heard. But rockets? They're deafening. They will hear them without a doubt!"

Pleading for support, Kovač tossed a nervous gaze toward the two lieutenants on the side of the room. Each of them knew better than to get involved.

"Who do you think made those rules, Kovač? Do you think they're out here today? Do you think they're taking a stroll outside that gate you busted down?"

The rat-a-tat-tat of the crew-served machine guns being fired in the valley below roared over the ridge and echoed in the small, metal structure. They both looked out the window.

Growing restless, Kovač replied, "It was the city council, sir. The city council voted to limit the loudest kinds of military activity at this site due to its proximity to the homes. They live in the city. Yes, they will hear the rockets!"

"NATO pumped over ten million dollars into this facility, Kovač. The city council doesn't set the rules here anymore. Hell, *I* don't even set the rules here," said the major, now impatient with the unruly Croatian. "We hardly ever use this place, anyway. I think they can put up with the racket a few times per year."

Kovač ran his hands through his hair as he racked his brain for a response that would satisfy the major.

"If we disobey those rules, sir, the Croatian Ministry of Defense will be forced to shut down military exercises altogether on this training ground. Please, I am begging you," Kovač pleaded as he held his hands in front of him in supplication.

"That's not going to happen, Kovač."

"There will be repercussions, sir! Do you know what this will mean for me?"

Refraining from replying, Major Meyers walked back to the window and raised the binoculars. Both sets of squads had now reached the positions from which they would set up the crew-served machine guns. The AT-4 rocket team would begin firing from cover near the wood line momentarily. He lowered the binoculars and turned back to Kovač.

"We're firing the AT-4s, Kovač. We're here to train to fight and win wars. There's nothing you can do to stop it. And you know what? If anyone complains, you can tell them you couldn't stop it," Major Meyers said. "It's out of your hands. I'm sorry."

Kovač felt a sharp chill travel down his spine as the cool, collected major took a step closer.

Leaning forward, the major said under his breath, "Frankly, I don't think anyone will be surprised."

Kovač's eyes welled with tears. He froze in his old, Croatian, standard-issue boots. He tried to speak but could not find his voice.

More machine gun fire came pounding over the hills.

"Won't be long now, Kovač," the major said, turning away. "I get it. It sucks. But this is all for you guys, anyway."

Kovač clenched his fists, and a rage boiled inside his heart. The major walked back to the window, raising his binoculars. The crusty first sergeant stood ready, watching from the back of the room, his face mangled with anger, seething at the gumption of the Croatian to question the major. Frozen in indecision for what seemed a lifetime, Kovač suddenly realized he had not yet heard the unmistakeable, piercing explosion of an AT-4 rocket launcher firing in the distance. Rousing himself from his paralysis, Kovač leapt toward the door. The first sergeant trained his gaze on him like a wolf. In a moment, Kovač was gone, and the door was again left swinging in the cold wind. Grabbing his radio, the first sergeant looked to the major for his next orders, and, without any hesitation, the major yelled for Kovač not to be allowed anywhere near the range.

"We're not letting that asshole shut this lane down for one minute."

Running out the door, Kovač saw his car parked haphazardly in the gravel, a reminder of the first real initiative, or rash decision, rather, he'd attempted in years. Rounding the corner of the building, the front of the range lied in sight at the bottom of a long, dirt road. He knew if he could just get to the bottom, the range safeties would be forced to call a cease-fire, and the range would go cold, giving him enough time to call his superiors and inform them of the situation.

Dreams of his new future quickly faded as he now hoped only to salvage his meager reputation. He struggled down the steep, uneven road, made slippery and wet by the heavy rains from the day before. Kovač knew he had only a few moments before the rockets would begin firing. His heart beat faster as seconds slipped away, and he did his best to sprint downhill in the grit and the mud.

Suddenly, as if out of nowhere, a strange noise grew louder in Kovač's ears, but it was no rocket. Continuing his uneasy dash downhill, he turned his head to catch out of the corner of his eye a running, screaming man quickly closing in on him from behind. Kovač picked up his pace, but his worn boots lacked the tread needed for the trail.

Almost instantly, the wily staff sergeant was on him. Tackling him from the back, the staff sergeant brought Kovač to the ground, and the two rolled boots over brow to the bottom of the road, landing in a muddy ditch, meters away from the front of the range. Scrambling to his feet, the staff sergeant grabbed Kovač by the neck and brought him back down into the mire, holding him in place as Kovač struggled to free himself. The old Croatian went limp as the first rocket fired from the wood line. The staff sergeant eased his grip and slowly stood up, looking at Kovač laying on the wet ground.

"What the hell is wrong with you, man? Were you trying to get yourself killed?" the staff sergeant screamed over the machine guns and the barrage of exploding rockets in the distance.

Kovač sat up, his face covered in mud and tears. Taking a deep breath, he shifted his gaze from the range to the man standing over him. The defeated Croatian extended his arm in the air, gesturing for aid, and the dreary skies poured rain again. After finding their feet, the staff sergeant and Kovač struggled their way back up the hill, Kovač limping in the sludge.

The Schnitzel and the Shark

Five heavy knocks thumped through the door, followed by a pause.

"Benett, it's Mick. Open up the door, man."

The young, brawny Benett didn't move. He sat motionless on his couch against the long side of his barracks room wall, surrounded by empty soda cans and a smashed X-box. He had soft, brown eyes and a face that rarely expressed the wide range of volatile emotions he'd recently been so prone to experiencing.

Five more knocks.

"Come on, man. Open up! It's Friday!"

Crumbs rolled off his shirt and fell to the floor as Benett stood up and shuffled his way toward the knocking. He opened the door a few inches and looked down at his short friend.

"I don't feel like going out tonight," he said drowsily.

"We're going out tonight, Benett. We're headin' into the field next week for a long rotation. Are you tellin' me you're ready for three weeks in Hohenfels Trainin' Area, that stinkin' place?"

Benett blinked.

"Three weeks?" he asked. "I thought we were only going for one?"

The short New Yorker looked left and right and then in a lowered voice said through his thick accent, "I have it on very good authority they're changin' it to three once we're out there. Haven't you seen the packin' list? Looks pretty heavy for only a week, don't it?"

"I haven't looked at it yet. I figured I'd pack over the weekend."

"Always waitin' until the last minute. Well, you aren't packin' tonight, Benett. Now, come on. Get dressed."

"Not tonight, Mick. I had a terrible day, and I just want to get some rest."

"I know exactly the kinda day you had, and that's precisely why you need to go out tonight," Mick replied as he leaned down and pushed his elbow against the door.

The door didn't budge.

Mick looked up.

"Seriously, Benett? Are you really gonna leave all the *Fräuleins* to me?"

Benett smirked.

"Yeah, that's what I thought," said Mick. "Now, open up this door and let me in!"

After a short hesitation, Benett stepped back and took his hand off the door, and as Mick triumphantly made his way inside, so did a heavy waft of cedarwood cologne. Walking toward the closet, he rubbed the palms of his hands together, determined to help his friend choose just the right shirt for the evening, but before he could, he was distracted by dozens of empty pizza boxes, glass bottles strewn across the tile floor, and piles of dirty laundry lying about.

"*Mein Gott*," he said, turning to face his embarrassed friend. "This place has really gone to hell."

"I haven't had much... time," Benett responded, scratching his head and avoiding eye contact.

"What if you bring a girl back here?"

"You know I'm not very good at that, anyway."

"Right...," Mick said. "Well, we can work on that tonight. Is that grey button-down of yours clean? The one with the pockets on the chest?"

"No, but it's fine," Benett replied as he grabbed the wrinkled shirt from the floor and held it up.

"Dude, I can literally see stains on that shirt from here. You're not going out in that. You live in Germany. Have you forgotten? Why are you acting like you live in Fort Leonard Wood or some other backwater?" Mick asked as he turned around and started rifling through his friend's clothes.

"Garbage," Mick muttered, throwing a shirt from the closet to the bed.

"Kitsch...."

Another shirt flew through the air.

"*Widerlich!*" he exclaimed as a third shirt was rejected.

He turned back to face his friend, who was now sitting, once again, on the couch.

"You need some new clothes, Benett."

"Why?"

"Because you need to start caring more about the way you look. That's important. Stop slouching all the time. That's important, too. It'll even make you feel better about yourself. And clean up your room, man. This is disgusting."

Benett looked away; his ears became red.

"I'm sorry, Benett. Come on. We're gonna have fun tonight," Mick told him as he picked out a random shirt from one of the piles of laundry. "Here, put this on and brush your teeth. I'm going to pull up my car. I'll meet you out front in ten minutes, and then we'll go to Regensburg for dinner and a few drinks. Okay?"

Benett still didn't want to go, but he knew that when this unlikely friend of his had set his mind to something, there was very little anyone could do to prevent it from happening. He feigned a timid smile.

"Okay."

***

After parking the car in a lot on the north side of the Danube River, the two started across the stone bridge with high barrier walls, whose sixteen medieval arches sat just above the water and led directly into the heart of the Old Town. It was a little before 7:00 p.m. on a cool night in spring, and the sun sat low on the horizon, casting its dim glow across ripples of blue and purple clouds that stretched across the sky above the town.

"I love this city, Benett."

"Yeah…."

"I mean, look at this place," Mick said as he pointed down the bridge toward the small city buildings of assorted pastel colors that sat below the watchful gaze of St. Peter's towering, grayscale, Gothic cathedral.

"We don't build cities like this anymore. It's a shame," Mick continued. "How does it make you feel, walkin' on this bridge?"

"What do you mean?" Benett asked, lifting an eyebrow.

"When I'm walkin' in Regensburg, I feel like I fit here. Ya' know, like a puzzle piece. Now, don't get confused, I love

New York, but it's built to the wrong scale. It ain't built for humans; that's for sure."

"I've never been to New York."

"Well, you oughta come sometime. I'll show ya' 'round the place, if I'm there. Kinda wanna stay here in Europe when I'm through with the Army, though. At least for a while."

Benett kicked a rock that skipped across the stones of the bridge while Mick cast his gaze down to the shoreline as the street lights began to flicker on, sending their warm reflections into the calm waters of the river below.

"Ya' know, it's a miracle all this is here right now," said Mick.

"Why?" Benett asked, his hands in his pockets.

"Back in the war, we bombed the shit outta Germany. Took plenty of cities to the ground. Sure, they got built up again, but it wasn't the same. Didn't have that old charm. But Regensburg made it through alright. The character, it was maintained. A truly medieval town."

Mick paused as the two arrived at the end of the long bridge. He looked up at a bell tower, sighing through a slight smile.

"*Momentaufnahme*," he continued as he looked back to Benett. "And now this city is a **UNESCO** World Heritage Site, protected, forever."

Benett didn't say anything. He simply listened to his friend tell him about a subject he had neither interest in nor enthusiasm about, but, regardless, he listened.

"Come on," Mick started. "I know a place down this way that has the best Bavarian food. We can sit by the water."

Benett followed Mick down a cobblestone path that ran between the city and the river. The already cool night grew colder as the sun continued to drop. As they walked, the cobblestone path slowly opened to reveal a stone courtyard centered on an ancient fountain surrounded by the tables and chairs of two opposing restaurants. Kids played by the river while their parents watched on from their candlelit dinner conversations. After the two friends were shown to a table near the fountain, Mick looked up and noticed Benett staring blankly at his menu.

"What kinda Bavarian food do you like, Benett?"

"I don't really know. I don't eat off-post very often."

"Can I make a suggestion?" Mick asked.

"Sure."

Mick leaned over the table and pointed to an item on the menu.

"*Semmelknödl*," he said. "Now, these technically aren't unique to just Bavaria. You can find them all over Central Europe, but they do them so well here."

"What are they?"

"Imagine giant meatballs. Like, really giant," Mick said, holding up his hands as if he were grasping something the size of a baseball. "But instead of meat, they're made of stale bread. This place stuffs them with pieces of sausage and cheese and boils them in a delicious meat broth."

He imitated a chef's kiss.

"Do they have pizza?"

"Where do you think we are, Benett? Italy? No, they don't have pizza. But if you're not in the mood to try somethin' new, they do make a good *Schnitzel*."

Mick could tell Benett was still confused.

"It's like a crispy chicken sandwich without the bread," Mick continued, "but in this case, it's pork. Know what I mean?"

"Yeah...," Benett replied, looking down as the waiter approached the table.

"*Guten Abend, Herr,*" said Mick.

"*Guten Abend,*" replied the waiter with a modest bow.

"*Okay, für mich, kann ich das Semmelknödl haben? Und für meinen Freund...,*" Mick said, pausing as he looked to Benett.

"*Schnitzel?*" Mick asked.

Benett nodded.

"*Und für meinen Freund, das Schnitzel.*"

"Okay," replied the waiter as he took the menus from the table.

"*Und zwei große Biere, bitte.*"

"Of course, sir," said the waiter with another bow of the head.

"Why did he reply in English?" asked Benett after the waiter had disappeared within the half-timbered, three-story home with a restaurant on the bottom floor.

"He knows we're Americans."

"How?"

"My German isn't that good, and it's pretty accented. And you, well, you look like an American," replied Mick with a smile.

"What gives me away?"

"It's never just one thing."

Mick looked across the river. By now, the sun had fully gone down, and all they could see of the opposite riverbank were shadows of buildings that seemed to be draped in a long string of clear Christmas lights.

"It's beautiful tonight, isn't it, Benett?"

"Yeah."

The waiter promptly returned to their table with two large steins of beer.

"*Danke*," Mick said.

The waiter bowed again and left.

"I didn't know you ordered us beers."

"I think it's late enough, don't you? *Prost*," he said, clinking his stein against Benett's.

"It's been a while since we've hung out, man," Mick said. "How have things been going in your platoon?"

Benett looked away.

"Things could be going better," he murmured under his breath.

"What's goin' on?" Mick asked, taking a sip of his beer.

"What have you heard?"

"Not much."

Benett glanced back at Mick, sensing his dishonesty.

Mick sighed and then took a drink of beer as Benett watched him.

"Alright. Well, I mighta heard you've been havin' a tough time fittin' in lately," Mick confessed. "And that you had a pretty rough day today."

"Who told you that?"

"I have a lot of friends over in third platoon."

Leaning back and looking across the river, Benett took a quick breath and started to speak but stopped before he had uttered a word. He shook his head and then looked back across the table.

"I don't know what I'm doing here, Mick. I don't think I can keep this up."

"Tell me what happened."

"It's my team leader."

"That blond corporal?"

"Yeah."

"What did he do?"

"It's never just one thing."

"Touché," Mick replied with a laugh. "So, what did he do today, then?"

"We were in the garages by the weapons room after coming back from the range," Benett replied after a pause. "I was carrying a 240 Bravo and had my M-4 slung over my shoulder. The strap slipped down my arm, and the M-4 hit the ground. When he saw that it was me, he yelled, 'Drop with it!' and then came running over and got right in my face, screaming at me to keep doing push-ups. Asked me if that was a proper way to treat a weapon and told me that because I don't know how to touch a gun, I shouldn't have the privilege of cleaning them. So he forced the team to clean my weapons while I sat with them and cleaned a broom."

"He made you clean a broom?"

"Yeah. Completely. Had to remove *every* particle of dust from the bristles. Had to unscrew the shaft from the brush cap and clean the gunk from the grooves. Had to scrub it with a toothbrush until my team finished cleaning all the weapons."

"It could have been worse, Benett."

"He knew some of the guys had plans to catch the 4:00 p.m. train to Berlin today. We were supposed to get off early. After they finished cleaning my weapons and turned them in, the team leader came over and inspected the broom. Said it wasn't clean enough. Made me break down the broom again and pass the pieces around to the team. Then we all had to clean the broom pieces for another hour. He released us after 5:00 p.m."

"So the guys missed their train?" Mick asked, looking behind his shoulder in anticipation of his *Semmelknödl*.

"Yeah. And they'd already paid for the hotel. I assume they'll leave tomorrow, but their big plans were for tonight. They know some girls there."

"You need to make it up to them, man. Make it right," Mick said between sips of his beer. "Take them out for dinner this week before we head to the field. You don't want to start the rotation off on the wrong foot."

"None of them would even agree to go out with me. They want me thrown off the team and put in a different platoon. Probably a different company if they had their way."

"How did things get so bad between you guys?"

"It's our damn team leader. He's great at dividing us. Aren't team *leaders* supposed to *lead*? Isn't the job description in the fucking title? This guy just wants to ruin my life, not lead soldiers."

"Do you think you did anything to catch his attention?"

Benett threw a puzzled look at Mick.

"What I mean to say is," he continued, "why is your team leader pickin' on you and not somebody else?"

Benett leaned back in his chair and shrugged.

"This guy is a shark, Benett. You know how they say a shark can smell a single drop of blood in the water from nearly a mile away? I don't know if that's true or not, but the principle applies," he said as he waved his finger in the air in the manner of a teacher.

Benett stayed quiet, staring at his beer, which sat untouched on the table in front of him.

"Listen, Benett. I've seen plenty of bad soldiers, and you ain't one of 'em. You hit a couple speed bumps in the road when you arrived in Germany a while back. You even admitted that to me once, right?"

Benett nodded, keeping his gaze trained on the table.

"Well, ya' caught your leadership's attention," Mick said. "You bled in the water, and now the sharks are circling, and things are spiraling out of control. You need to stop the bleeding, man."

"But I don't know how," he responded desperately. "Whatever happens, my team leader finds a way to either blame me or make me pay for it. And he turns people against me."

"You've gotta stop the bleeding, Benett."

Bennet sighed and then spoke up.

"Remember last month when that dude in fourth platoon blew through a crosswalk and hit a German?" he asked.

"I do," Mick replied.

"He was scheduled for a twenty-four hour CQ shift at battalion that night. Obviously, he was pretty busy with the MPs and the German cops, so he couldn't make his shift."

"He was drunk, by the way," Mick interjected. "He's probably gonna be tied up with the German cops for while. At least, that's what I heard."

"Think he'll go to jail?" Benett asked.

"No doubt."

"I can't imagine being locked up over here."

"On that, we can agree," Mick said as he raised his beer and took a sip.

"Anyway," Benett went on, "when CQ found out he wasn't going to make it, battalion sent out requests to all the platoons, asking for last-minute support, and, wouldn't you know, next thing I know, I'm being voluntold to fill his shift. Thing is, I was just getting off from an already long day because I had an early morning assignment to clean the company facilities for first sergeant's change of responsibility ceremony."

"That sucks, Benett."

"That's not even the worst part."

"What else?"

"The next day, when I got off the shift, I was exhausted. Went back to my room and took my uniform off. I turned on some music and then crashed on my couch. Woke up to my team leader and a buddy of his *in my room*. I thought I was dreaming. He was yelling at me, but I couldn't understand anything he was saying. By the time I realized what was happening and the words began to make sense, I heard his buddy screaming, 'Are you not going to stand at parade rest while a non-commissioned officer is talking to you?' I sprang off my couch and snapped to parade rest. Then I realized I was only wearing my underwear. He told me that someone in the hallway had complained about the music coming from my room. That was bullshit. I could smell the alcohol on his breath and knew he was drunk. Then he smoked me for twenty minutes right there in my own room. Burpees and push-ups until I could barely stand. Told me that if anyone else

The Schnitzel and the Shark

complained, he'd come back and smoke me for thirty more minutes. They left my room laughing."

"I'm sorry, Benett. That's tough. Really."

The two looked up as the waiter arrived at their table with the food.

"The *Semmelknödl* for you and the *Schnitzel* for you," the waiter said, lowering the plates to the table.

"*Danke.*"

"You have not touched your beer, sir. Do you not like it?"

"Oh, no, no," Benett replied. "I'm just not very thirsty yet."

"I understand. And you, sir?" he asked as he turned to Mick. "Would you like another beer?"

"I'd love another. *Danke.*"

The waiter bowed and left.

"You're not wrong," Benett said. "This does look like the chicken from a crispy chicken sandwich. Just flatter."

"I'm sure you'll like it; everything at this place is good," Mick replied, taking the first bite of his meal.

"How's your... your...," he started to ask, then paused.

"*Semmelknödl*," Mick said.

"Yeah. How is that?"

"It's absolutely perfect. Want a bite?" he asked, raising his eyebrows.

"I'm good with my pork. This is delicious," replied Benett as he chewed. "Thank you, though. And thank you for bringing me out tonight. I needed this. I needed to vent."

"I know ya' did. Everyone's gotta blow off some steam now and again. You're gonna be okay, man. Focus your energy on what you can control. Don't waste your time worrying about things you can't change. Like that ass-hat team leader of yours. Don't worry about him. This is the most authority he's ever gonna have in his life. Don't worry about little people."

"I know.... But it's hard sometimes. When he was walking out of my room that night, all I could think of doing was beating the shit out of him. Just landing two or three good punches. Draw some blood. Make him pay."

"And what would that accomplish?" Mick asked.

"It would put him in his place. And it would make me feel better."

"It wouldn't. And then you'd land yourself in a world of trouble. Don't tempt yourself with those thoughts, Benett. You hear me? It's a dangerous road. Don't run down it."

"You're right, Mick."

Mick leaned back and looked around among the many diners near them.

"These Germans, man. Ya' know, they have a word for everything. The most specific concepts get their own words in the German language."

"Really?"

"You ever hear of the word *Schadenfreude*?"

"No, I haven't," replied Benett. "What's it mean?"

"It's when someone takes pleasure in someone else's pain. It's a twisted sort of joy."

Benett stopped chewing and looked up from his meal.

"There's a defense against it," Mick continued. "Works every time."

"And what is it?"

"Don't give 'em the satisfaction. Don't show 'em how much they're gettin' under your skin. Don't let the sharks smell the blood."

Benett nodded, slowly.

"I'm just trying to help you, man. I know this stuff can be really hard. Ahh, here we are," Mick said, seeing his beer arrive.

"You ever gonna drink that beer of yours?" Mick asked Benett after the waiter delivered his drink and again departed with a bow.

Benett grabbed his stein and raised it up.

"*Prost*," he replied, a smile on his face.

"Hey! Very good, man!" Mick cheered as the two clinked steins. "To Regensburg."

"To Regensburg."

"Let's see what this city has in store for us tonight," Mick said before tipping back his beer and slamming it down on the table.

***

The two walked down the small, winding roads of Regensburg as the last of the diners ceded their territory to the oncoming waves of college students and all assortment of young people ready to play a role in the medieval city's buzzing Friday nightlife. Dinner tables were taken off the streets and replaced with round, hightop tables and the accompanying heat lamps that took the bite out of the cold air. The combination of the breeze on Benett's face and the alcohol he'd drunk to catch up to Mick awoke the recluse to a vision of the city he'd never seen before. A vision of life he'd never considered before. He watched the participants of the growing crowds mix in and around each other, weaving their way toward the bars and carrying their drinks back to the tables.

He turned his face from the bars and the cafés to his friend walking beside him, a duo as dissimilar in size as in disposition.

"Where are we going to stop, Mick? These all look great to me."

"Wherever you want. You decide."

They came to a busy cocktail bar at the end of the block, the busiest one in the area. It sat on the corner where the street gave way to the square. People spilled from the arched, stone entryways of the bar into the historic platz centered on another fountain.

"Here. Let's stop here."

"Looks good to me," Mick said as he nodded his head and cracked his fingers. "I'll head in and grab some beers. You find us a table."

Benett politely pushed his way through the sea of people until he found a table that had just been deserted. He quickly claimed it and waited for Mick. While he waited, he couldn't help but notice two girls, who were standing at the table next to his, drinking cocktails from ornately-designed, glass flutes. They were too close for Benett not to not make eye contact with the one who stood opposite him. He nodded in her direction, and she smiled back. He ran his eyes down her long legs to her feet, which met the cobblestone in black, high-heeled boots. His heart beat in his throat, and his ears grew as red as her lipstick. Shaking his head and looking down, he bit his lower lip and closed his eyes.

He took a deep breath and then sprang up, looking straight in their direction.

"Hello!" he screamed above the constant din of the crowd.

Met with the abrupt and unexpected greeting, the two girls stopped their conversation and quickly turned their gazes toward Benett. Their surprised faces signaled to him he might have made a mistake.

"Umm, hello...," the one with the red lipstick and blonde hair said through a laugh.

"You're American," said the other one.

"Yes, I'm an American," he said as he nodded his head in relief, an awkward smile on his face.

"Are you alone?"

"No, my friend is inside, getting beers."

"You work at one the American bases, or are you tourists?"

"We do work at base. How did you guess?" Benett asked.

The two girls glanced at each other, fully aware of how obviously soldier-esque Bennet appeared to anyone looking. A moment later, Mick arrived at the table holding two large beers.

"Hello, ladies. How we doin' tonight?"

"We are doing well," the one with short, brunette hair and a leather jacket replied enthusiastically. "Do you want to join us at our table?"

"I think we'd love to join you ladies. *Danke*," Mick replied as he put his hand on Benett's back and pushed him toward their table.

"Your German is very good," the brunette woman said with a playful smile.

"Ayy, well, I appreciate that very much, but I do know more German than just *danke*," he replied as he set his beer on their table.

The girls laughed.

"What do you two do at the American base?"

"I'm a photographer," Mick said, placing his hand on his chest, "I go all over Europe, takin' photos of what the U.S. is doin' here."

"This is very interesting. I did not know there were photographers in the Army."

"Of course. The Army has a place for everybody."

"And you?" the blonde woman said as she looked at Benett.

Mick put his hand on Benett's shoulder.

"Benett here is a stone-cold killer, a brute, a damn war hero," Mick said as Benett smiled, his ears still red.

"How long have you been in Germany?"

"I've been here for a few years. Love the place. Benett, on the other hand, still pretty green. He's been here less than a year."

"And do you like Germany?" the blonde woman asked, looking at Benett again.

"I love Germany," he screamed.

The girls rocked back on their heels as Benett glanced away, his ears turning an even brighter shade of red.

"I love the architecture here," he continued in a lower voice. "I'm glad the city made it through the war."

He coughed as the girls looked at each other, slightly confused by his odd answer.

"Yeah," the blonde woman said. "Regensburg is very beautiful."

"Oh, and I really like all the words you have in your language. Words for really specific ideas," Benett said as he looked at Mick.

Mick winked.

"And what is your favorite word?" the blonde woman asked.

"My favorite word? It's, umm, it's shadden... shaddenfroiy...."

"*Schadenfreude?*" she asked with a questioning smile.

"Yes, that's the one! Great word."

"Why do you like *Schadenfreude*? It is such an ugly idea, no?"

"See, didn't I tell ya' that Benett was a stone-cold killer?" Mick quickly added.

The girls laughed, but their laughter was interrupted by the reactions of the crowd to a bald man in a tank top rudely pushing his way toward the bar, stumbling as he went.

"Blood and honor!" he screamed.

"*Shiza*," whispered the brunette.

The girls looked at one another, an annoyed expression on the face of the brunette. Several in the crowd raised their phones to record the bald man.

"Who's that?" Mick asked. "And is he sayin' what I think he's sayin'?"

"He is saying what you think he is saying," the blonde woman said. "And in English this time, so he does not go back to prison."

"Prison?" Mick asked.

"He just got out. He used to wander around Regensburg on busy nights, protesting and trying to make fights with people."

"What's he protestin' about?"

"He protests many things," she continued. "The European Union, the millions of refugees that Germany accepted from *Syrien* and *Irak*, our bad politicians."

She paused, looking at Mick and Benett.

"And the American bases," she said quietly as she hunched her shoulders forward.

By now, more of the crowd had started filming. Others had already called the police.

The four of them watched as the bald man with leathery skin and a raspy voice intrusively stumbled toward the bartender, people moving out of his way lest they be accosted. The bartender raised his voice and aggressively pointed toward the door.

"What's he sayin'?" Mick asked.

"The barman is telling him he is drunk and that he is not welcome here. The man is asking why he will not pour a drink for his German brother."

The brunette woman brought her hand to her mouth in shock as the bald man pounded his fists on the table and spit in the bartender's face.

"*Mein Gott,*" said the blonde, looking at the man with soft eyes full of pity.

Wiping the spit from his face, the bartender walked out from behind the bar. He approached the bald man and grabbed him by the neckline of his tank top. In a quick motion, the bartender reared his head and swiftly head-butted the bald man onto the ground. A collective gasp rose from the crowd that had formed around the scene.

"Holy shit," Mick exclaimed. "This is quite the show, ain't it, Benett?"

Benett only watched. His eyes showed a deep interest so unlike his typically straight-faced expression.

"*Wie schrecklich*," the blonde woman whispered to herself.

The bartender picked up the bald man and threw him out the open, arched stone door. He landed among the crowd, and, as he rose to his feet, people quickly stepped away. Laughing as he moved forward toward the square, he locked eyes with Benett, whose height set him apart from the others.

"Mick, I think he's looking at me," he said worriedly.

"Stop talkin', Benett," Mick whispered.

Hearing the English, the bald man approached their table like a moth to a light. The girls grabbed their purses and moved away.

"We don't want any trouble, man," Mick said.

"You do not want trouble?" the bald man replied as he laughed. "Okay. No trouble. Tell me. You are tourists? Because, to me, you look as soldiers."

Benett and Mick remained silent, staring back in horror at the man whose blood dripped from his forehead, down his face, and onto his tank top.

"I think your silence means you are soldiers," he said in a frustrated, heightened voice as he raised his arms above his head and looked around him at the faces in the crowd.

"*Sag es mit mir*," he yelled, trying to rally the people who'd now formed a large circle around them.

Raising his wretched voice, the bald man screeched, "Germany is not American colony! Germany is not American colony! Germany is not American colony!"

Despite his best efforts, he could not convince anyone to join him in the chant. They only watched in disbelief. He stepped within inches of Benett as the tall American leaned backward in repugnance and fright, his heart beating out of his chest.

"Don't do anything, Benett. Just stay calm. Let this guy have his fun, and then he'll move along," Mick advised.

"Yeah. Don't do anything, Benett," the bald man mocked. "You do not want to have fight you cannot win."

He slowly raised his hand to Benett's scrunched face and touched his opponent's forehead with a finger.

"I bother you, Benett?" the bald man asked before Mick stepped between them, bumping the man back a step.

"Move along, man. That's enough. You've had your fun. Now leave us alone," Mick asserted.

The bald man stared at Mick with wide, incredulous eyes.

"We are not American colony! We are not American colony!" he shouted as the two Americans stepped back.

The man drew in a short breath and then spit across Mick's face, screaming, "Go home, colonizer! *Das ist Deutschland!*"

Benett drew back his arm as Mick screamed for him to stop, but before Mick could intervene, Benett threw a punch at

The Schnitzel and the Shark

the bald provocateur, who easily dodged the poorly thrown fist and responded by tackling Benett to the ground. The crowd gasped. Mick rushed to the aid of his friend and pushed the bald man off, but not before the man had landed two or three punches to Benett's face, drawing some blood. The bald man jumped up. Cries of "Polizei! Polizei," rose from the crowd, prompting him to dash away toward an alley. German police descended on the scene as the crowd chaotically dispersed. Mick helped Benett up, and the two ran off, down the road and toward the bridge from which they came. When they reached the river, they stopped running.

"What the hell just happened?" Benett asked Mick through panting breaths.

"You just started a fight. That's what happened."

"No, I didn't! That asshole did!"

"Not on paper, Benett. You threw the first punch, and there's about fifty witnesses who saw it."

"I didn't even land it," he said as he grabbed his jaw. "I think he might have broken something in my mouth."

"Come on. Let's just get outta here quick," Mick said. "You can get it checked out on Monday. Tell 'em you tripped comin' down the stairs or somethin' like that."

As the two began crossing the bridge, leaving Regensburg behind them, Mick looked up at Benett.

"I'm sorry I didn't throw him off you quicker, Benett."

"I know you were there as fast you could have been."

"Well, I still feel bad. And it was my idea to bring you out tonight. All so you could get your ass kicked!"

Benett laughed, looked forward, and then stopped in his tracks.

"Mick, there he is!" he frantically whispered as he pointed down the bridge at a bald man walking away from them on the left side, near the high, stone barrier. "He must have grabbed a jacket from someone."

"I don't know if that's him, man."

"Oh, that's him, alright," he said as he sprinted ahead of Mick.

"Benett, stop!" Mick yelled, running after his friend.

Approaching the bald figure from behind, Benett violently pushed his victim against the stone barrier of the bridge. His head bounced off the stone like a rag doll, and he fell to the ground, blood pouring from a gaping cut above his right eye.

"Remember me, Nazi?" Benett screamed as he mounted the fallen man and raised his fist high.

In a single moment, as his fist hung in the air, the vengeance and rage vanished from Benett's ravenous eyes, and his expression turned to one of pure terror and regret.

Panting and out of breath, Mick caught up to his friend.

"That's not him, Benett! What have you done?"

The Schnitzel and the Shark

Red Sheepskin

Rain drizzled over the ancient city of Athens. It was a cool, grey evening in autumn, and a dense fog had moved in from the sea and settled over the cars, people, parks, and plazas of the sprawling urban center. Tucked into a dark corner of a café sat a stocky, bald man of middle age. A filter in wait between his teeth, he gently rolled the contents of a packet of rolling tobacco into a cigarette paper as he watched passersby scurry to and fro under the wet weather to their various activities and appointments. He wore a black, leather jacket, and as he switched on a lighter to light the cigarette, a long scar from his temple to his jaw became illumined on the left side of his face. Across his forehead lay the wrinkles of a man whose eyebrows had long been accustomed to a resting state of furrow. Paying for the beer he had drunk, he drew several euros from his pocket and set them on the table.

"*Efcharistó,*" he said in his low, raspy voice, thanking the waitress as he passed her on his way out the door.

He walked toward the sidewalk and stopped just before reaching the street. Taking a drag of his cigarette and exhaling the smoke into the fog, he lifted his head to the low-rise complex of apartment buildings that stood across the way, plants and drying clothes adorning the balconies that extended from the concrete facade.

"*Ena, dyo, tría,*" he said under his breath as he counted the floors of the building.

His advancing eyes rested on a single balcony. He squinted. The apartment behind the balcony looked warm; its light glowed orange. A young man, who played a guitar and bore a striking resemblance to him (save the baldness, wrinkles, and scar), came into view. He watched him for several moments and slowly became aware of a jealousy that tugged at his heart, connected by an invisible cord to a freshly resurrected memory of his youth. He brought the cigarette to his mouth again, only to discover that the rain had drowned it out. Flicking it into the street, he returned his gaze to the balcony, where a beautiful woman with dark, brunette hair had joined the guitarist. She watched him play against the backdrop of Athens and the bad weather, smiling at him as she swayed to the rhythm of his song. The man on the sidewalk blinked his eyes and ran his hand across his face to wipe away the raindrops that flowed like a small river from the top of his bald head, through his scar, off his chin, and into the street.

Motorbikes and busses passed in front, but the fortitudinous man didn't budge. His gaze remained fixed on the couple above though he was now quite wet. He stayed for a good while until something inside of him had had enough, at which point he stepped off in the general direction of the city center, leaving the warm apartment and memories behind him. Down that famous thoroughfare called Leoforos Vasileos Konstantinou, his legs followed his high, stiff shoulders, passing the oft-vandalized statue of Harry Truman and then taking a right toward Hadrian's Arch and the ruins of a Roman bathhouse. As he drew closer to the center, the city's pulse beat faster, and the rain gradually ended.

The man hadn't walked these routes in over thirty years, but at no point did he need to stop and reorient himself. He knew exactly where he was going, and he was reminded of his smoke-filled experiences on these very streets in distant years: chaotic student riots, clashes with police, and demands for Greece to unplug from the influence of the American hegemony.

He'd felt like an imposter in those days, but he couldn't speak about it with anyone, even the one he'd loved in those early years —before the scar, before many things. He had maintained the belief that he didn't have all the answers and didn't know what the right path forward might look like. Complicated times.

Upon reaching the small hotel where he was staying, just north of the Greek Parliament, he walked inside and crossed the gilded hotel lobby, adorned with sculptures of the gods. After passing the check-in desk, he immediately felt a pair of eyes train in on him from somewhere by the couches in the corner. Waiting for the elevator to open, he tried to catch a glimpse of his watcher in the gold-tinted doors' reflection, only to see that the individual in question had since left the couches and was now walking up behind him.

"Lieutenant Colonel Olethros?" he heard from behind.

"Yes?" he replied in his low voice as he turned.

"I'm Staff Sergeant Eric Kim," the man with sharp facial features and thick, black hair fashioned in a high and tight said as he reached his hand forward. "Your acting drop zone safety officer."

"Oh, Kim. I thought you weren't getting in until tomorrow."

"The Air Force guys moved my flight left, sir. I got in this afternoon."

"Well, it's good to meet you," Olethros replied, looking down and to his left in his typical manner of talking with people. "Have you checked into your room yet?"

"Yes, sir. I have."

"You can drop the 'sir' for now, Kim. Especially when we're in public and out of uniform. Operation security and all that," he said in a quieter voice as he looked toward the various sections of the lobby. "Don't always know who's listening."

"Whatever you'd like," Kim replied.

"Follow me to the roof. There's a bar up there. I'll buy you a drink."

The pair took the elevator together and, after arriving at the bar, sat down at a table with a view of the Acropolis, which sparkled like a distant heaven through the small amount of fog that still remained. Between them and the hill on which that pinnacle of classical architecture stands was a complex maze of cheaply constructed concrete and soulless structures, neoclassical buildings and homes, and various remnants of ancient ruins, preserved where they were discovered.

A waiter approached their table.

"I'll have a Hellas beer," Kim said after skimming over the menu.

"*To ídio tha écho parakaló,*" said Olethros.

Kim looked at Olethros with a puzzled expression as the waiter nodded and left.

"You speak Greek, sir?"

Olethros glanced at him sideways.

"Sorry," Kim said and then coughed. "You speak Greek?"

"I am Greek," he replied as he gazed at the Acropolis. "I left this country for the United States thirty years ago. This is my first time back."

Kim raised his eyebrows.

"Wow," he said. "Is it nice being home again?"

"I don't know yet," Olethros replied, looking down and to his left. "Where are you coming from? You're stationed in Germany with the airborne cavalry, aren't you?"

"That's right. I'm in Graf with the 91st. Coming in from Spain, though. I was DZSO for a small airborne op with the Spanish paratroopers this week."

"I heard about that exercise. Busy summer for the brigade."

"Seems like that's the way it goes for this brigade. Always on the move."

"Always on the move," Olethros quoted back to him a bit satirically as he lifted his quickly delivered beer. "This exercise, though, it's a different beast."

"How do you mean?"

"It's not your typical rat race. We're not running around, shooting lasers at opposing force or trying to outcompete a NATO ally. Hell, we're not even really training at this one."

Kim looked at Olethros inquisitively.

"This is more of a dog and pony show," Olethros continued. "Every once in a while, the big guys like to see what their militaries can do. They like to see NATO allies working together. Blowing shit up and knocking down doors. Combat ready and hooah. We're not just increasing interoperability here; we're proving it to the people who matter."

Kim nodded his head.

"Who's going to be here for the big day?" he asked.

"There's going to be some very important people here," Olethros replied. "Very important."

He paused, seemingly losing track of the conversation as his eyes once again drifted toward the Acropolis.

Kim waited in the awkward silence.

A few seconds later, Olethros returned to the conversation.

"Well, the ambassador will almost certainly be there. Some other Americans from the embassy. Maybe a few Greek members of parliament. Probably a couple generals. Kind of a mixed bag with exercises like this. Who knows who could show up."

He paused, taking a sip of his beer.

"Who knows who could show up," he stated again, looking down and to the left.

"Where are the troops staying?" Kim asked.

"The company is staying in barracks at a training base across from the airfield you flew in on. It's not much, but it was easier to put them there. Don't need to figure out daily transportation back and forth from Athens to the training grounds. We'll drive up there tomorrow, and I'll introduce you to the company commander. Then you can take a look at the drop zone."

"Roger that," Kim replied.

***

The next morning, the pair drove deep into the countryside of Central Greece to a training base that sat unassumingly within a patchwork of farms and hilly pastures. Pulling into a small gravel lot that sat atop a plateau above a lea, they parked their car and walked through the area, busy with workers installing portable bleacher seating, toward several men in U.S. Army camouflaged uniforms standing at the precipice and watching groups of soldiers training below them several hundred meters away. As Olethros and Kim neared the edge, the men shifted their attention from the soldiers in the distance and brought their rigid right hands to the corners of their eyebrows in salute toward Olethros.

"Good morning, sir," one of them said cheerfully through his salute, an eager look in his blue eyes.

"Isn't this technically the field?" Olethros replied, looking at the rural scene that surrounded them. "And besides, I'm not in uniform, so you can drop those salutes, gentlemen."

"Very well, sir," the one who had spoken first said, shaking Olethros' hand as the others in the group returned to watching the soldiers far away and below them.

"Bauer," Olethros said, "this is Staff Sergeant Eric Kim, our DZSO. Kim, this is Captain Bauer, the company commander of the soldiers here for the exercise."

"Nice to meet you, sir," Kim said to Captain Bauer, who nodded back at Kim.

"How have the Greeks been treating you?" asked Olethros. "I'm sorry I haven't been out here in a couple days. The barracks alright?"

"The Greeks have been great, sir. No complaints from us toward them. The barracks do get cold in the evening, though. But we're infantry. We've dealt with much worse."

"Good," replied Olethros, looking down and to the left and then shifting his gaze toward the soldiers below them in the grassy area. "Tell me what we've got going on over here. You think the troops are ready for tomorrow? Some very important people will be here."

"I think we're ready, sir. We've been hard at work preparing for this," Bauer said as he pointed his hand toward several makeshift wooden structures in the distance. "This is the area the Greeks and our MP dog handlers will clear first. That group will arrive on Greek helicopters and then go building by building, reacting to the opposing force."

"And then where do you guys parachute in?"

"It's difficult to see from here, sir, but can you make out that hill on the horizon?" Bauer asked, with his hand pointed up and to the left of the makeshift structures.

"I think I can see it."

"That hill is just north of a very small landing strip over which we'll execute our airborne operation and then establish a perimeter. When we've secured the strip, the Greeks will start landing aircraft with supplies, food, and medical personnel to attend to the notional local population. Once the area gets transformed from a combat zone to a place suitable for a humanitarian mission, it's done. End of the exercise."

"This is the drop zone?" Olethros asked, pointing to the area near the hill far behind the wooden structures.

"That's right, sir."

Olethros turned to Kim.

"Want to go check it out and make sure it's all set for tomorrow?"

"Right away, sir."

Olethros turned back to Bauer, looking in the direction of the group of soldiers near the makeshift buildings.

"Looks like they're about to take one of the buildings," said Olethros. "Can I borrow those binoculars?"

Bauer handed over the binoculars that had been hanging around his neck, and Olethros lifted them to his eyes.

There were three cheaply constructed, wooden buildings. About a dozen notional enemy forces, having already been dealt with by the combination of Greek and U.S. soldiers, lay on the ground around the building nearest the plateau.

Olethros focused on the next building. Five soldiers with rifles were stacked against the long side of the wall, a foot away from a door. The man at the front of the stack had a dog at his side. The second man had a stun grenade. A third soldier walked toward the door with a shotgun, pointed it at the handle, and shot it with what Olethros saw to be a forcefully projected bean bag. After being blasted by the bean bag, the thin, plywood door bounced open as the second man leaned past the first and tossed in the flashbang. The team waited for a few seconds until the device went off, and the first man took his hand off the collar of the dog. It dashed into the building. The team of five quickly followed. Olethros heard the sound of several rounds of blanks fired in quick succession and then observed a brief pause. A moment later, Olethros saw the dog jump out the window of the short side of the building, kitty-corner to the side the team had entered from. If the dog's jump through the window could be described as graceful, the same could not have been said of his handler, who misjudged the height and caught his feet on the bottom ledge of the window. He tumbled forward and landed clumsily on his butt on the ground outside the building.

Olethros' heart sank as he watched the incident unfold. He sighed, slowly, maintaining his focus on the team as the rest of the soldiers exited through the same window and joined the other group of soldiers providing perimeter security and moving toward the next building.

"Seems like the MPs have a *little* more work to do," said Captain Bauer ever so sarcastically, followed by a nervous chuckle.

Olethros closed his eyes and exhaled. He lowered the binoculars and turned to respond to Bauer, but before he could utter a word, his sunken heart was thrown into a frenzy as his veins were instantly filled with adrenaline. He didn't move. He didn't even breathe.

"Sir?" Bauer inquired. "Everything alright?"

There was no response from Olethros, whose eyes were locked in on something behind Bauer.

Captain Bauer turned around. A man in a formal, Greek military uniform stood by the open door of an idling car. He was the object of Olethros' gaze, as Olethros was the object of his. The man in the Greek uniform swallowed and then nodded. Unfastening the buttons of his blazer, he ducked into the back seat of the car and gave Olethros a final look before closing the door.

"Do you know that guy, sir?" asked Bauer.

They watched the car drive down the road that led off the plateau and into the farmland.

"Sir? You know that guy?" repeated Bauer. "I think he's one of the officers heading up some of the logistics and planning on the Greek side of the exercise. Not sure, though. I haven't spoken with him, but he's been in and out of the training grounds all week."

"Yes," Olethros slowly replied as he watched the car wind through twisting roads. "I believe he's tasked with something like that."

"Did you meet him at the planning conferences for this exercise, sir?"

"No, he wasn't at the planning conferences."

A short period of silence ensued as Olethros was yet again caught up watching the car drive away. Bauer did not know what next to say. He broke the silence with a cough and then a question.

"Will you be joining us this evening at the officer's club, sir?"

"Joining you for what at the officer's club?" Olethros asked, gradually returning to his conversation with Bauer.

"The Greeks have decided to throw us a party at their officer's club in the village down the road. They said there will be dancing and *ouzo*, whatever that is."

"I might show up," replied Olethros, still not fully present. "No promises, though."

***

That night, the company of visiting American soldiers joined the Greeks at a *taverna* on a cobblestone street in the sleepy village just down the road from the training base.

"Remember, we're representing the United States and the entire brigade," Captain Bauer told his soldiers before they arrived. "Let's be on our best behavior."

As they walked in, the Americans found a handful of Greeks plucking metallic noises from stringed, wooden instruments with long necks. The music was upbeat and, to Bauer's ear, seemed more oriental than Greek, but, then again, this was his first time in the country.

The soldiers packed the whole place full, including the outdoor courtyard in the back. It was dark, but a large fire blazed from within a stone fireplace in the corner. On the mantel sat several old copies of *The Iliad* and *The Odyssey*, much of the works of Hesiod, Plato, and Herodotus, and newer books as well, like the many travel memoirs of Nikos Kazantzakis, held up by bookends carved in the shape of doric columns. A large table had been set full of plates of roasted and seasoned tomatoes, fried potato wedges, and cuts of meat with names the Americans had never heard before: *souvlaki*, *apáki*, and *gyro*. The air smelled of dill and garlic. There was pita bread, yellow rice, wine, and, as the Greeks had promised, there was *ouzo*.

The hosts welcomed their guests warmly and took great pride in showing off their food and music. The first time a circle of dancing Greeks formed in front of the musicians, the Americans were hesitant to join. But after a few glasses of *ouzo*, which many of the Americans drank as shots rather than following the advice of their allies—"*Pietíte argá*. You must drink slow, my friends"—the Greek and American soldiers soon found themselves shoulder to shoulder, arms around each other in a circle, kicking their feet forward and back as the group rotated to the beat of the instruments.

"Is called *bouzouki!*" shouted a man over the noise of the music.

He had deep wrinkles in his face and slicked back, grey hair. His old, leathery skin was tan and dark.

"What?" one of the American soldiers replied.

The man emulated with his hands the way one holds and strums a small ukulele and then leaned in toward the American he had cornered.

"*Bouzouki!*" he repeated.

The pungency of the alcohol on his breath forced the American to shrink away in a moment of disgust. He looked back. The Greek stood waiting, a happy, drunken smile on his face.

"Oh, the instrument!"

The old Greek nodded and then was caught by surprise as a friend of his crashed into the conversation, throwing his arm around his neck.

"*Ti les se aftó to paidí,*" the newest member of the conversation slurred to his friend. "*To bouzoúki eínai tourkikó órgano. Írthe stin Elláda me tous Orthódoxous Toúrkous metá ton ellinotourkikó pólemo. Eínai tragodía pou to chrisimopoioúme!*"

"*Aftó den eínai alítheia!*" the man shouted back, visibly concerned by his friend's comment. "*Ítan i ellinikí diasporá pou tin éfere píso stin Elláda, óchi oi Toúrkoi!*"

The man who had interrupted the conversation, also quite old, rolled his eyes at his friend and then looked at the American.

"He's drunk!" the Greek screamed.

"So you are!" his friend shouted back.

The American stood watching as the two Greeks burst into laughter.

The first Greek turned to him and yelled, "If Ottoman menace want fight, I join army again and spit in the eye!"

"We will crush them with the help from American friend we have here!" the other Greek shouted as he clenched his fist and raised it in the air triumphantly.

"I don't really know what you guys are talking about, but if someone's coming after you, we've got your back!"

Hearing the confirmation from the American, the face of the second Greek grew serious. His tone became somber.

"Yes, you do. Because the enemy of your friend is your enemy," he said to him. "Remember that, American. Loyalty is more precious in this world than all the gold of King Midas."

Caught by surprise, the barely nineteen-year-old American soldier simply nodded.

"Now," continued the second Greek, "say it with me: *Alala!*"

"*Alala*," said the American.

"No, scream it!"

"*Alala!*" shouted the American, his glass of *ouzo* in the air.

The two Greeks cheered.

"*Alala!*" they called out.

"What does it mean?" the American asked.

"It is the war cry of our ancestors. They screamed it as they ran into battle against the Persian and the Ottoman, winning back what was stolen by those ancient enemies of our freedom."

"I had no idea Greece had been through so much."

"Since the fall of Constantinople," the second Greek continued, "the Hellenes have endured much. Unlike your revolution fought over taxes, the survival of our people depended on victory."

"That's awful," the American commented, now bashful and unsure of his place in the conversation.

"It was long time ago," the Greek responded, moving his head from side to side. "We will see."

The trio was standing near the fire. As the Greek finished speaking, he motioned for the American to follow him to the mantel, where he selected an old, hardcover book from the eclectic collection. The old man flipped it open and read aloud about a seldom discussed crime in the town of Merzifon, from the anonymously authored *Black Book; The Tragedy of Pontus, 1914-1922*.

"I had family here," he uttered before he read. "But that line has ended."

> *The scenes which took place in the course of the fire were heart appalling. All the exits are barricaded, and the miserables trying to escape, are either mercilessly killed, or thrown back into the fire, without distinction of women, children and old men. In the lapse of five hours 1800 houses together with their inhabitants, were burnt down. It is impossible to describe the orgies committed against the virgins and children. While they were performing these cruelties, they shouted at their victims, "Where are now your English, your Americans, and your Christ to help you?"*

When the man finished, he looked up and locked his sad eyes with those of the anxious and unsettled American standing in front of him.

Late in the night, after much dancing, drinking, and conversing, Captain Bauer told his platoon sergeants to gather the soldiers onto busses and take them back to the training base. The soldiers were in good spirits, and when they returned to the barracks, they played music from a portable speaker one of them had brought along. The drunkest ones sang karaoke and danced. The captain watched from his bunk at the end of the barracks hall, laughing quietly to himself. Out of the corner of his eye, he saw a figure he thought to be an unassuming Lieutenant Colonel Olethros step into the hall. The soldiers in the immediate area noticed him but didn't know who he was. Bauer sprang off his bunk.

"Company, attention!" he shouted. "Good evening, sir."

The soldiers in all four halls of the barracks jumped off their beds and stood at the position of attention. They paused the music. Everyone looked at Olethros, whose timid smile calmed the tension on the faces of the closest soldiers.

"Relax, everyone," came his low, raspy voice. "Relax."

The soldiers eased up their positions of attention, but remained quiet, watching him.

"Please, everyone, relax," he said as he walked down the hall toward Captain Bauer.

"Good evening, sir. How can we help you?"

"Evening, Bauer. Sorry to bother you guys in your barracks so late. How was your party?"

"It was a good time, sir. Would have loved to see you there."

"I probably should have shown up, but I'm glad you had a good time," Olethros replied, looking down and to the left. "I stopped by tonight to chat with the MP who stumbled out the window earlier this afternoon. Is he here?"

"Yes, sir," Bauer said, an eyebrow raised. "I think the MPs are in the corner of the hall three down from ours. I can show you there, sir. Is he… in some sort of trouble?"

"Absolutely not. I just want to talk with him, if that's okay."

"Of course, sir. Follow me."

Bauer led Olethros down to the third hall, into the corner where the borrowed MPs were staying. Soldiers quieted their voices and stood up straight as the lieutenant colonel passed their beds.

"Here are the MPs, sir."

"Thanks, Bauer," Olethros said, nodding his head. "You can go back to your bunk."

The MPs all stood at attention.

"Relax, guys. May I sit down?"

The MPs eased up.

"Yes, sir," one of the MPs said, gesturing toward a bed.

Olethros took a seat as the MPs stood around him.

"No one's in trouble or anything, fellas. I'm just here to chat. So, which one of you guys tripped coming out the window this afternoon?"

Five of the six MPs looked at the one in the middle. The one in the middle looked down.

"Then it was you, huh?"

"Yes, sir."

Olethros looked at the five others.

"Do you guys mind if we borrow this area for a little while? Do you have somewhere else in here you could hang out?"

The five other MPs nodded and left. The sixth remained standing, concern on his face.

"Relax. Take a seat."

The MP sat down on the bed across from Olethros.

"That was quite a tumble you took coming out the window earlier today. Are you alright?"

"Yes, sir," the MP quickly replied. "I scraped my shin pretty bad, but I'm fine, sir."

"Do you trip often?"

"No, sir. I don't trip often. I think I just misjudged how far the window was, sir. I was focusing on the dog."

"Do you think it could happen again tomorrow? Do you think you need to run through that building a couple times in the morning, just to practice and make sure you're ready for the window?"

"I think I'm ready, sir. We ran through the scenario a few more times after the iteration where I tripped, sir."

"Good," Olethros replied as a smile appeared on his face. "You're ready, then! Ready for the big day."

"Yes, sir."

"Because there's going to be some very important people there tomorrow. We're not just showing off. We're explaining that the American machine and the NATO alliance is good, *strong*, and there's nothing else like it in the world. Never has been."

"Yes, sir," the MP replied.

Olethros could tell the boy was still uncomfortable.

"Are you nervous?" he asked.

"Yes, sir. I don't have many conversations with lieutenant colonels."

"Listen, man," Olethros replied. "We put our pants on one leg at a time, just like you. Sometimes we even lose our balance while doing it."

The MP laughed.

"Yes, sir," he said.

Olethros looked behind his shoulder and then lowered his voice.

"To tell you the truth, I actually feel more like a joe than an officer."

"Were you ever enlisted, sir?"

"I was never enlisted in the Army, but I'd done a few things before I found my way to West Point."

"What were you doing before West Point, sir?"

"That's a conversation for another night," Olethros replied, looking down at the floor and to the left. "But I've been an officer for a long time, and I've made the U.S. Army my home, but I've never shaken the feeling that I'm some kind of imposter. Masquerading among the officers, where I'm not supposed to be."

He was again reminded of the student riots and the way he felt there, among those students who all seemed so committed and sure of their ideas.

Olethros looked back up and made eye contact with the MP, who, although confused at the direction of the conversation, maintained a professional tone and posture.

"How old are you?" Olethros asked.

"Twenty-two, sir."

Olethros laughed.

"Twenty-two," he repeated. "You've got a lot of life left in front of you. You have a girl?"

"No, sir. I don't."

"If you find a good one, listen to her."

The MP nodded.

"I'll try, sir."

"And don't fuck up the window jump tomorrow," Olethros said as he stood to leave.

The MP stood quickly.

"I promise, sir. We'll execute the raid flawlessly."

"I know you will."

Olethros patted him on the back and then turned to leave. As he neared the hall with the drunk soldiers and their still-paused karaoke, Captain Bauer called the company back to attention. Olethros turned around. All the soldiers watched him.

He hesitated and then slowly spoke up.

"I'm very proud of everyone here. You've all done a great job training for this exercise. Tomorrow is the big day. There's going to be some very important people watching the exercise. Get some rest. Goodnight."

With those parting words, Lieutenant Colonel Olethros turned back toward the door and left the building.

***

The next morning, Olethros arrived at the training grounds early. He dropped Kim off at the drop zone and then drove to the larger landing strip across from the barracks, where the troops were putting their parachutes on and jumpmasters were inspecting each soldier to make sure the parachutes were ready to deploy. After ensuring the Air Force had arrived on time with the C-130 and one last check-in with Captain Bauer to confirm he and his company of paratroopers were ready to go, he drove back to the plateau.

It was busy. Dozens of cars parked neatly in the gravel lot. VIPs had already begun arriving and taking their seats in the bleachers, which overlooked the makeshift, wooden structures, the drop zone, and the small landing strip. Large monitors had been set up around the plateau so that when the exercise began, the spectators could watch a live stream from several GoPros attached to the helmets of soldiers engaged in the action.

Introductory graphics composed of text and fire displayed on the many massive screens. A French guest whispered to his colleague about how realistic they were, far superior to the graphics on the screens of the Turkish exercise the two Frenchmen had attended the previous spring.

Olethros scanned the faces in the crowd. There were well over one hundred people on the plateau. He recognized many from the planning conferences.

"Well, there's the ambassador," he mumbled to himself. "There's the Greek military attaché to our embassy."

He kept scanning, almost frantically. He checked his watch.

"There's still some time," he said under his breath.

Pulling out his cell phone, he sent a text message to Staff Sergeant Eric Kim.

9:53am

Everything good to go out there?

9:54am

All good out here, sir.
Drop zone ready for an airborne operation

9:54am

Good

He looked back to the crowds of people, searching the faces of the different groups. Momentarily, he caught a glimpse of a brunette woman in a long, black dress walking toward the bleachers from the parking lot with a group of Greek officers in formal uniforms. He strained to see her again, but she was near the back of the group.

Was that her? Olethros asked himself.

Everyone's attention was captured by the sound of three Greek helicopters that quickly swooped into view above the plateau, kicking up a great cloud of dust among the VIPs and the officers watching. The men reached for their hats to secure them to their heads and prevent them from being blown off, while the wives of the VIPs took hold of their dresses. The helicopters landed in the grass on the opposite side of the plateau from the wooden structures. Greek soldiers and the U.S. MPs emerged onto the field, weapons drawn and a dog at their side. They moved tactically toward the wooden structures, crossing in front of the plateau. The VIPs were captivated. Those with poorer vision watched the live stream. Others watched the small, distant soldiers move across the field with their own eyes.

The group of Greek officers and the brunette woman had found seats in the bleachers. Olethros had kept an eye on them as they moved but didn't want to draw their attention by looking directly at them. Now he had a clear line of sight toward her profile. That was her. He was sure of it. His palms sweated, and his heart throbbed as he watched her from the side of the bleachers, his position obscured by the railings.

Olethros looked up. He heard the faint sound of a C-130 incoming toward their position. The paratroopers were on their way. He looked back at the woman in the bleachers to see if she was watching.

The crowd gasped, signaling the first actions taken by the teams of Greek and U.S. soldiers nearing the makeshift buildings in front of them.

As the teams approached and some of the opposing force emerged from the first building, one of the Greek soldiers threw a smoke grenade at the door. Olethros became suspicious. He didn't know a smoke grenade was going to be used in the firefight for the buildings.

A plume of red smoke issued from the burning grenade and drifted swiftly toward the sky.

Olethros panicked.

"Damnit!" he yelled to himself as he sprinted toward the designated Greek safety officer, who sat on a ledge above a short ladder in a type of tree stand assembly at the end of the plateau.

When Olethros got to the stand, he grabbed the bottom of the ladder and looked up at the officer.

"Is that part of the exercise?" he screamed.

"What?" the man in the stand shouted down to him.

"The red smoke," Olethros yelled back. "Is the red smoke part of the exercise, or is the drop zone actually unsafe?"

The C-130 full of American paratroopers was now directly overhead. Its volume, the noise of the crowd, and the several bursts of gunfire from the soldiers on the ground made it difficult for the Greek to hear and understand the frantic American.

"Wait," the safety officer hollered down to Olethros, pointing up at the plane above them both.

Olethros grunted and then turned his head toward the drop zone. A quiet laughter percolated among the crowds on the plateau as the C-130 passed over the drop zone with no American paratroopers in sight. Olethros was furious. He turned back to the safety officer in the stand.

"Is the red smoke just for camouflaging the position of the Greek soldiers on the ground as they attack the buildings, or is the drop zone not safe?" he screamed.

"The red smoke is part of the exercise. The drop zone is safe. Your paratroopers have missed their target."

Olethros threw his sweaty, shaking hand into his pocket and grabbed his phone. He immediately called Staff Sergeant Kim.

"Kim!" Olethros shouted.

"Yes, sir?"

"Did you cancel the jump?"

"Yes, sir. I did."

"Radio the jumpmaster and the pilots again. Tell them to circle back and exit those paratroopers!"

"But, sir, there's red smoke in the area. That means the drop zone isn't safe."

"I know what it means, Kim!" Olethros cried. "But it was just part of the exercise! I confirmed it with the Greeks. Exit those paratroopers!"

"Roger, sir."

Olethros hung up the phone and turned, shaking where he stood, to watch the C-130. Seconds later, it began turning around and coming back toward the drop zone. He sighed in relief but remained quite nervous. He looked to the bleachers and saw the VIPs focused, their gazes fixed on the incoming C-130.

As the plane passed over the drop zone, Olethros saw one paratrooper exit from the jump door on the side that was facing him. A parachute deployed within seconds, and the soldier was suspended in air, slowly drifting down toward the drop zone. Another paratrooper emerged, then another, and another. Within a minute, the C-130 had passed the drop zone and two platoons of American paratroopers stretched out across the sky, falling softly to the ground beneath large, olive drab parachutes.

"Alright," Olethros said to himself. "Now it's up to you, MPs."

He walked back toward the bleachers and stood in a spot from which he could watch one of the monitors without being seen by the woman in the black dress. The Greeks and Americans had just entered the second building. Shots rang out. Out of the window jumped the dog.

Olethros bit his lip.

"Come on, man," he whispered.

A second later, the twenty-two-year-old MP jumped through the window, landing next to his dog. The rest of the team followed. They moved to the next building, where only a small contingent of the opposing force was left. By the time the company of American paratroopers had secured the air strip by the hill at the end of the field, the three makeshift, wooden buildings had also been cleared of combatants.

The Greeks began landing aircraft on the small landing strip. A forward operating base was set up alongside a casualty collection point and a field hospital. The entire area was transformed in minutes before the VIPs' eyes. Role-players portraying a local population were routed through administrative checkpoints and given food supplies and medical attention for any notional injuries or illnesses. Several more planes landed, bringing notional NGO workers, who set up schools and created wells and other infrastructure necessary for sustaining life.

Olethros was impressed with the attention to detail the Greeks had paid this portion of the exercise. It was a greater display than had been discussed at the planning conferences. As the operation concluded, the VIPs saw a thriving society, rebuilt from a chaotic combat zone in less than an hour.

Organizers prompted the VIPs to exit the bleachers and make their way to the back side of the plateau, where ten Greek special forces soldiers stood in full battle rattle: helmets, night vision goggles, eye protection, armor, and weapons at the low-ready. Rucksacks full of gear sat on the ground in front of each of them. A guide explained the different aspects and functions of their gear and uniforms to the VIPs in the Greek language while a second individual translated what he said into English.

Not everyone watched the presentation. Others roamed around the plateau, talking with colleagues or checking out different views of the training grounds.

Olethros weaved through the people, looking for the woman in the black dress.

She was right there in the bleachers only moments ago, he thought. *How could she have slipped past me? Did she already leave?*

"Vassilis Olethros," came a voice from behind him.

He turned around. There stood the man he'd locked eyes with the day before. They paused.

"I always knew we'd see each other again, old friend," Olethros said, looking at the ground and to the left.

"*Triánta éna chrónia chorís léxi kai tóra mou milás angliká?*" the man asked.

"*Den miló schedón kathólou elliniká edó kai treis dekaetíes,*" replied Olethros.

"And it shows," said the man. "Fine. English, then."

He smiled somberly at Olethros.

"How have you been?" Olethros asked.

"Is that really what you want to ask me?"

Olethros glanced up and looked straight into the man's eyes. He spoke and then stuttered. Unable to continue, he looked down again.

"Is she happy?" Olethros forced himself to ask.

"I think she is," the man responded. "I hope so."

"Family?"

"We have two kids."

Olethros let out a quick gasp and then recomposed himself, nodding, still staring at the ground.

"I'd always assumed you two would find your way to each other, but I never knew for sure."

"You left, Vassilis. We both knew you were never coming back. What was she supposed to do?"

Olethros looked back up at his friend.

"How much does she know?" he asked, his voice lower and coarser than normal.

"She knows we had some involvement with NATO," the man replied, "but she doesn't know the details. I don't think she even knows what a stay-behind unit is."

"Did *we* even know what it was in the beginning?"

"We learned quickly."

"Does she hate me?" Olethros asked.

"You can ask her that question yourself," the man said, raising his chin in the direction of the parking lot. "Go on. Talk to her."

Olethros turned toward the vehicles. Standing at the edge of the lot, watching them, was the brunette woman in the black dress. He walked to her. As he neared, he could tell she had been crying. Her eyes were still wet, and her makeup was smudged across her face.

"Maia," Olethros said slowly. "You haven't changed at all."

She gazed at his face, finding her composure.

"You only speak English now?"

"I've spent the last thirty years with the Americans," he said. "My Greek is not what it used to—"

"You disappeared overnight," she blurted out before he finished his sentence. "For years, I thought you were dead."

Olethros was taken aback by the almost cold resignation in her voice.

"I had to leave. And it wouldn't have been safe for you to know where I was going," he replied with the same emotionally divorced tone.

She looked him up and down.

"It's true, then," she said. "You ran off and joined the American military. Just when things were starting to turn around here."

"And you married a career soldier," he shot back.

She scoffed.

"There were many things these last few decades that did not go the way I planned," she replied. "That is life, right?"

She focused on his scar, prompting him to look down and to the left to hide it from her view.

"How did you get that?" she asked.

He nodded toward the exercise, indicating warfare as the cause of his injury.

"From dealing with some really bad people," he finally answered.

"You don't believe any of this, Vassilis. This is a show. A *theater* performance meant to make us feel okay about living in a corrupted system."

Olethros swallowed and turned his head back toward Maia.

"Sounds like its not just your looks that haven't changed."

"I haven't been fooled, Vassilis. Or moved away from what we all used to believe," she replied, coldly, staring unflinchingly at him.

Disappointment shot through his stomach like a barrage of Persian arrows, and a knot formed in his tightening throat. He accepted the loss and realized that the MP could have stumbled out the window and it wouldn't have made a difference.

"I'm sorry I left like that, Maia, all those years ago. I never meant to hurt you."

And with those parting words, Vassilis Olethros turned and walked away.

Red Sheepskin

Pavlo's Horror

Five men crouched in the woods, near the edge, where the trees gave way to a clearing. The sun had not yet risen, but it was close. The men had been there all night, silent and still. They were waiting for the perfect moment to attack.

Of the five, three were Americans: one sergeant, a specialist, and a private. Their features were obscured by camouflage face paint. They wore tactical vests and combat helmets. The other two were Ukrainians. The older of the pair was named Igor. He was thick and dense, but not in good shape. He had been in the Ukrainian military a long time. His face was calm. Nothing riled him up. The younger soldier was named Pavlo. He was the opposite of Igor in many ways: skinny, jumpy, and on edge. His eyes were bloodshot, and he gripped his rifle with a ferocity that could have strangled a small animal.

In the middle of the clearing stood an old, wooden house. It was unpainted and dilapidated. On the porch were two men in black military uniforms. They were smoking cigarettes, and they were greatly looking forward to the end of their shift, soon as the sun came up. One had a rifle slung over his shoulder. The other had set his rifle against the side of the house. A Russian T-90 battle tank sat squat in the grass, scars of warfare scattered across its shell, as it guarded the house from a short distance.

Back in the woods, the men gathered around the American sergeant, who took off his gloves and began quietly explaining the attack strategy a final time on his palm. The plan was simple. At the right moment, the squad would jump from the forest and descend on the guards while a second squad, only meters down the wood line, would address the tank. A third squad would be seconds behind the first two, stacking on the door of the house and clearing it.

The sergeant motioned for the men to lean in close to him.

"Alright," he whispered, "intel says the weapons cache is inside this house. We've only seen three guards all night. Should be an easy target. Let's keep it tight. Destroy the guards and the tank. Grab the weapons. Back at the FOB by breakfast."

He glanced around him at the men kneeling in the dirt. They were stoic. All but Pavlo, whose eyes darted from side to side while sweat beaded on his forehead and rolled down his face. There was something in Pavlo's expression that a sent a shiver down the sergeant's spine. He pulled the gloves back over his hands and turned to Igor.

"Does he understand the plan?" the sergeant asked, referring to young Pavlo, who spoke no English.

"He understands," Igor replied, patting Pavlo on the back.

The sergeant took another look at Pavlo and then turned away.

"Glad that guy's on our side," the sergeant whispered to the other two Americans as he moved back to face the clearing.

He slowly lowered a mouthpiece that was attached to his helmet and an earbud.

"Second squad, you ready?" he murmured.

"Ready, sergeant," he heard through the earbud.

"Roger. Third squad?"

"All set, sergeant."

"Roger," he replied.

He turned to the men of his own squad and motioned for them to creep as close to the wood line as possible, which they did, being careful not to step on any branches that could snap and give away the element of surprise.

With a quick flick of his wrist, the sergeant signaled to his squad, and they leapt from the woods and sprinted toward the house in the clearing, their weapons raised and ready to engage the enemy soldiers on the porch. The other two squads, emerging from slightly different points, were directly behind them.

The tired soldiers on the porch were shocked into action, throwing down their cigarettes. The one with the rifle on his shoulder raised the barrel, but before he could fire a round, he was overrun by the American sergeant, who shot him three times in the chest. The enemy combatant fell to the porch. The second soldier dashed toward his rifle but was gunned down before he reached it.

As second squad surrounded the tank, a third soldier in the same black uniform ran out from behind the house, rifle in hand. Pavlo saw him first and instantly raised his weapon at the incoming soldier, firing a single shot. The soldier in black was struck in the head and collapsed onto the ground.

"Nice shot, Pavlo," the American sergeant yelled out.

Pavlo didn't move or acknowledge the praise.

First squad established a perimeter of security around the house and tank. Third squad stacked on the door. Pavlo didn't move. In fact, he barely breathed, staring at the soldier on the ground whom he'd just shot.

Second squad threw a grenade inside the hatch of the tank, rendering it useless, as third squad broke through the door and began clearing room after room. As it was a small house, the squad very quickly found it empty of people, but full of weapons.

Finally, Pavlo moved. He dropped his weapon and inched forward in the direction of his victim.

Turning from his position on the security perimeter, Igor noticed something was wrong with Pavlo.

"*Pavlo, ty dobre?*" Igor asked.

No response.

Pavlo approached the third guard and stood directly over him. Pavlo's eyes were bloodshot and wide, as they had been all morning. With a guttural shriek, Pavlo dropped to his knees, grabbed the unmoving man by the collar, and punched him in the teeth. Having been hit unexpectedly, the guard flashed open his eyes in shock and anger.

"What the hell are you doing, man?" the guard cried as he tried to wrestle his collar from Pavlo's grip.

With his free hand, Pavlo wound up and punched the man again, this time with a primal scream that caught the attention of everyone in the area.

The safety personnel, who had been standing at the edge of the scene, rushed toward the brawl.

"Do not hurt him! He is having a panic attack!" Igor called out after he threw down his gun and chased after the safety personnel.

By the time Igor arrived, the safeties had separated Pavlo from the role-player and moved them to opposite sides of the house. The guard, who had been struck a third time before being rescued, was spitting out blood and screaming obscenities at a shaking Pavlo, who was surrounded by safeties.

When Pavlo saw Igor gently push past those standing around him, he erupted into a fit of tears as he crashed into Igor's embrace.

The other two men in black uniforms got up and checked on their fellow guard while all three squads of infantrymen stood at a distance and watched old Igor rock Pavlo back and forth in his arms and whisper calmly into his ear.

Nobody knew exactly what to do, least of all the safety personnel, who shared inquisitive looks with one another as they waited for Igor to let Pavlo go.

When that finally happened and Pavlo had begun to calm down, one of the safeties approached Igor.

"What did we just witness?" he asked Igor, out of earshot of Pavlo, now sitting on the ground and leaning against the side of the house.

"He only returned from the frontlines a few months ago. He has not adjusted well," Igor replied. "I am sorry for your man. Pavlo is small, but he can throw a punch."

The safety looked confused.

"The frontline?" he asked.

"Yes. The civil war in Donbas against the Russians and the rebels."

The safety furrowed his eyebrows and leaned in toward Igor.

"You're telling me that young man was fighting actual Russians only a few months ago?"

"Yes. This is what you do when you are at war with Russia. You fight actual Russians," Igor responded.

The safety was visibly taken aback. He looked over at Pavlo, still leaning against the side of the house but now taking controlled, deep breaths again and again.

"You have forgotten there is a small war raging on the other side of Europe, haven't you?" Igor continued as he put his hand on the safety's shoulder. "It is okay. Many have forgotten. But if you travel through Moldova and drive east past the Dnipro River, you will find a war zone."

"What should we do with him?" the safety asked.

"The game is finished for Pavlo, I think, yes? I will withdraw as well, to stay with him."

The safety nodded.

"I'll drive you two back to the rear and find you a place to sleep," he said. "When you get settled, I'll notify your commander of where he can pick you up when the exercise is over and the units start leaving."

"Thank you," Igor replied.

He turned toward the group of guards in black uniforms, who had gathered on the porch.

"I am sorry for your face!" he called out to the one Pavlo had punched. "He was not in his right mind."

"I understand," the guard replied as he rubbed his jaw, having come down from the adrenaline and now realizing Pavlo was likely experiencing some flashback or an episode of post-traumatic stress disorder.

After nodding his head toward the remaining members of first squad, Igor called young Pavlo to his side, and the two Ukrainians followed the safety to a car and quickly left the exercise and the wooden house in the Romanian forest behind them.

This wasn't the first time Igor had to explain to someone that Ukraine was in a protracted war. The ones that drag on are easy to forget.

As the Romans

The automated voice of the bus announcement system interrupted her diligent study of a travel guide to the city of Rome that was siting in her lap. She capped her highlighter and looked out the window as the bus turned a corner and approached a station.

"*Stai arrivando a Roma Termini.*"

She checked her watch. "Thirty-seven minutes late," she said to her herself as she started nervously tapping her fingers on the guide.

"You are now arriving in Roma Termini. Please gather your belongings and prepare to depart."

She huffed. Closing her travel guide and turning a page in her notebook, she ran her eyes down a long list of sights and activities she had scheduled for herself.

She scrunched her nose and scratched her head.

"Which one of you gets knocked off the list…?" she whispered.

Taking a pencil from the bun of black hair on the back of her head, she brought it down to her notebook and paused just under item number seven of day number one: Eat cannolis at *La Cannoleria Siciliana*.

Looks like I'll go from the osteria directly to the Colosseum. That will have to do, being that I'm already running late, she thought as she crossed out the cannolis from her list.

She stood on her tiptoes to reach her brown, leather weekender-bag from the overhead compartment and then quickly put her notebook and travel guides inside.

The bus stopped, and the doors opened. Everyone began shuffling toward the exits.

She was a fit woman with a runner's body. Dark, large-frame glasses sat in contrast against the light brown skin of her small, round face, and she wore boots with a tan blouse over black jeans.

When she stepped off the bus and walked out of the station, she found herself in a busy Rome, bathed in summer sunlight.

Item number one: a late lunch and an espresso, she thought.

A block-long building of white stone stood across the street. The bottom floor held *trattorie*, bars, and stores within a colonnade of arches separated by Doric columns.

And this will do splendidly.

She crossed the street and took a seat at an open table in the sun. Taking out her phone, she refreshed her email inbox. Twice. And then she checked all of her different text and messaging apps, just to make sure she didn't miss a notification in a stretch of bad cell service while on the bus. She put her phone away and let out a long breath.

Rome, she thought. *The Eternal City. It does have a charm, doesn't it?*

A waiter approached her table.

"*Prego*," he said.

"*Ciao. Per me il panino tonno e olive e un caffè*," she responded, accented but perfectly correct.

"*Bene. Un panino con felino. Lo preferisci tritato e messo nel panino o a parte?*" the waiter asked, speaking very quickly and using words she was not familiar with, although she felt she had a competent grasp of the Italian language.

She raised her eyebrow at the waiter, asking, accented but correctly, what he meant by his question.

The conversation caught the attention of a man in his early thirties sitting two tables away, who had seen her walk from across the street minutes earlier. He watched with a smile, knowing exactly what the root of her confusion was. An old Fujifilm camera hung off his chair. He had brown, curly hair that he kept short on the sides and slightly longer on top, and he wore loose khakis with a white, button-down shirt. It was still early in the summer, but it was clear he'd already spent much time in the sun, as he was thoroughly tanned.

As he listened to the conversation, he began to wonder about who the woman was.

She is clearly not backpacking, but she came out of the station by herself, so she is probably not just a regular tourist, either, he thought. *And her Italian is far too good to be one of the foreign students.*

His interest was piqued.

The conversation continued between the woman and the waiter, with little to no progress being made.

She is very pretty, he thought, leaning back in his chair and biting a pen he kept in the pocket of his shirt. He was both drawn to as well as repulsed by her, and, like the source of the confusion he was currently witnessing, he knew exactly what the reason for it was. *What might she be doing here?*

After his curiosity had gotten the best of him and he could no longer keep himself away from the beautiful young woman, he slowly got up from his table, slinging the camera from his shoulder and walking toward the woman and the waiter.

"*Vuole il panino senza il gatto,*" he said to the waiter, who, upon hearing the interventionist, smiled and abandoned his fun.

"I told him you just wanted the sandwich," he continued, looking down at the woman sitting at the table.

"Thanks," she said, turning toward him. "I thought my Italian was getting pretty good, but I had no idea what that guy was saying."

"That is because he was speaking Romanesco," he replied. "It is a little different than Italian."

"Oh? He doesn't speak Italian?"

"Yes, he does. But the waiters here like to play with tourists getting off the trains. It is not a nice thing to do, but it is accepted at this bar."

"In that case, thank you. Thank you for stepping in. That was nice of you."

"You are welcome," he replied with a smile. "May I sit down, or are you expecting company?" he asked, placing his hand on the back of the chair across the table from her.

She looked surprised.

"Umm, no," she spluttered as she grabbed the fabric of a belt loop on the right side of her pants and nervously passed the denim material between her thumb and pointer finger. "I'm not expecting company, but I can't stay long."

"You have plans in Roma?"

"Yes," she replied proudly. "Many. And I'm already running very behind. The bus was late getting in."

He laughed.

"You must be prepared for this when you are traveling in Italy," he said. "The trains can be even worse."

A *different* waiter approached their table with a sandwich and an espresso.

"*Grazie,*" the man with the camera said to the new waiter.

The waiter paused from setting down the plates and looked up at the man.

"*Ah, siete italiani,*" he said. "*Non lo sapevo. Questo caffè fa schifo. Torno subito.*"

He left the sandwich and then quickly turned on his heels and vanished with the coffee behind one of the doors of the block-long building of white stone.

The woman raised her eyebrows high. She turned to the man with the camera.

"Did he just say the coffee was shit? But only after he realized you were Italian?"

"This bar gets mostly tourists. Now, because of my accent, he knows I am from here and assumes you must be too."

"What would I have found in that coffee?" she asked, a horrified look across her face.

"Nothing serious, only shitty coffee. They re-use the beans. Tourists cannot tell the difference."

"I guess that's two things I owe you for," she replied.

He was happy to hear her say that. Being quick on his feet, he capitalized on the good will he'd earned.

"In that case, now, may I sit with you?" he asked.

She let out another long breath.

"Fine," she said. "But only for a little while. I have a very busy day planned, and I can't fall too much further behind."

"You may leave whenever you want," he replied, pulling out the chair and taking a seat. "I am Federico."

"I'm Araceli," she said as she shook his hand. "*Piacere.*"

"*Piacere,* Araceli. That is a beautiful name. We have it here, too. Where are you from?"

"Mexico, but I came to the United States with my parents when I was a baby."

"Do you speak Spanish?"

"It's all we spoke at home. I didn't learn English until I went to school."

"Funny," he replied.

She tilted her head and squinted her eyebrows.

"He probably didn't learn Italian until he went to school," Federico said, nodding is head in the direction of the first waiter, who'd just approached the diners at a nearby table. "Romanesco is likely his first language. Italian, his second. That's common around here."

She peered at the waiter, a gentle look in her eyes.

"I would never have guessed it for you," Federico continued. "You speak English with nothing of an accent. And your Italian, it's very nice."

"I still have a lot to learn," she replied, looking back at Federico.

"What brings to you Roma, Araceli?"

She quickly scanned her surroundings.

"It's complicated," she said. "Short answer is that I'm just a tourist here for the weekend."

"I love complicated," he replied. "What is the long answer?"

"Long answer is that I was forced to take a vacation. My boss told me I've been over-working myself. We have a stressful summer ahead of us, and he wanted me to take a break before everything gets crazy, so here I am," she said, raising her shoulders and clacking her tongue.

"You are with the American military, aren't you?" Federico asked.

She sat up in her chair, her posture quickly changing from relaxed to defensive.

"Why do you ask?"

"I am very good at noticing these things, even when it is not *too* obvious. And the end of your military I.D. is sticking out from your wallet," he said as he pointed to her belongings on the table.

"How do you even know what this is?" she questioned, grabbing her wallet and pushing the I.D. fully inside.

She looked at him with sharp eyes.

"Do not worry," he said. "I am not dangerous or anything. My mother worked at the U.S. Navy base in Napoli. She was a cook in one of the cafeterias. I grew up around a lot of Americans."

"Oh," she replied softly as she looked down, feeling bad she'd gotten visibly defensive now that she knew the innocent reason he could identify her.

"Let me guess," he said. "United States Air Force?"

"Army," she responded, a small smile appearing on her face as she started to relax her posture again.

"Then you must be stationed in Vicenza, or are you over in Pisa?"

She hesitated, but then said, "I'm in Vicenza."

"How long have you been here in Italy?"

"Around nine months."

"Very nice," he said. "I hope you are enjoying this country. It has much to offer."

"I like what I've seen. It's beautiful in the north. Haven't been south of Florence."

"But you have been here so long. And you have not traveled outside the north?"

"Work has kept me busy," she responded, starting to feel more comfortable around him. "I have an unusually demanding job."

The second waiter arrived back at their table, carrying, presumably, an espresso made with fresh coffee grounds.

"*Grazie,*" both of them said to him.

"*Di niente.*"

After the waiter left, Araceli leaned in toward Federico.

"About that first waiter," she said, looking behind her to make sure he wasn't walking through the door, "what was he trying to say to me earlier? Something about a cat?"

"He was asking if you would prefer your complimentary side of cat meat cut up and put in the sandwich with the tuna, or separately, on another plate."

She lifted the left side of her upper lip in disgust and then looked down at the sandwich that had been sitting on the table for several minutes.

"That doesn't look so appealing to me anymore," she said, nodding her head.

Federico laughed.

"Tell me, Araceli, what are your plans for your weekend of forced relaxation here in Roma?"

She pulled out her notebook.

"I've compiled three lists of items I want to see and do in Rome, broken down by how much I want to do each thing. The first list is for things I absolutely want to do here. The second list is for things I'd like to do but don't need to do. And the third list is for things I'd like to do, but only if there's extra time within the respective geographic zone. Each item has been assigned a number that corresponds, roughly, to how much time a given item takes to complete. Obviously, I prioritized the items from the first list. But, when I accounted for time as well as location, I compiled a single, optimized list that maximizes the number of items I can complete in a single weekend, with as many items from the first list as time could be allotted for."

Federico stared back at her.

"And this is how you plan to relax in Roma," he said ironically.

"I'm sure it seems like a lot, but I don't know if I'll ever be back here. I mean, the world is a big place. Maybe this is my first and last time in the city. I need to make the most of it."

"What is your job in the Army?" he asked.

"I'm a logistics officer."

He laughed faintly.

"What?" she asked.

"I believe if I had thought about that question for more than two seconds before I asked it, I would have arrived at the answer myself," he said as he watched her take the first sip of her espresso.

She looked down at the table, hiding a spontaneous smile when she heard his quip.

"May I try the coffee?" Federico asked. "To make sure it is fresh."

Araceli handed him the cup, and he took a very small sip, savoring it and moving it across his tongue.

"This has certainly been made with fresh beans," he said. "*Bene.*"

When he passed it back to her, her fingers brushed across the side of his hand. Their eyes met across the table. She glanced down. He watched as she brought the plate to the placemat in front of her, doing her best to avoid looking him in the eyes again.

"You... like to take pictures?" she asked, nodding toward the film camera he'd slung on the back of the chair.

"I do," he said. "It is maybe the thing I like to do the most. Or sitting in a bar and watching the Roman afternoons turn into evenings."

"What do you take pictures of?"

"Mostly the Roman afternoons. The Cyprus trees. People walking back to work after quickly drinking coffee in the bars. How the light falls on the ruins in the Forum. The cats."

She looked at the sandwich and raised her eyebrows.

"Not the ones that become sandwich meat," he continued.

He looked out toward the street in front of them. Araceli snuck a long glimpse of him as he watched the people walking past. She thought his crooked teeth were cute.

He turned his face back toward her.

"Araceli," he said. "I do not believe a strict adherence to your list will make a relaxing weekend for you."

"And why do you think that?"

"Roma," he said, picking up her notebook and holding it, facing her, in the air, "cannot be reduced to a simple checklist."

She looked at him suspiciously, but, secretly, she was quite amused at his audacity.

"Continue," she said.

He smiled.

"You must be patient with her. You must pay her what she is due. Walk her narrow streets without a destination in mind.

Many people visit this city every year. They go to the museums, eat the pizza, take a picture by the *Fontana di Trevi*, but they do not know Roma when they leave. Despite their efforts, they never met her while they were here."

"How do I meet this Rome you speak of?" she asked, humoring him but very certain of the effectiveness of her own method. "Am I supposed to just wander around aimlessly, hoping I bump into an experience or a person or a meal that's going to introduce me to some idyllic, fantastic version of Rome?"

"Like all good things, this takes time. Maybe it takes a day. Maybe it takes a year. But it cannot be accomplished with a checklist."

He leaned back in his chair.

"Besides, you did 'bump into' me while ignoring the constraints of your checklist, did you not?" he continued. "Maybe I am the person who can bring you to the genuine Roma."

She looked around her and then took a full sip of her espresso, finishing it.

"And what would we do?" she asked, taking another long breath and looking back at him as she grew slightly anxious at just the thought of straying from what she perceived as a list of responsibilities.

"You are missing the point," he replied serenely.

She tapped her fingers on the table in front of her, looking at him with something of a glare.

He reached for his camera.

"May I take your photograph?" he asked.

"Why?" she scoffed, reaching apprehensively for the fabric of her favorite belt loop.

"Usually, the light around mid-day is quite ugly. I hate it. But today, the light, how it reflects from the stone of the building and shines on your face..., it is very nice. I do not think I could pass this moment without taking a photograph of you."

She looked at the table. Slowly, she brought her hand to her hair to re-adjust it.

"No," he said abruptly, stopping her in the process. "Do not change anything."

She brought her hand back down to her lap and straightened her posture, looking toward the camera as he turned the lens and moved backward to focus on her face.

"I think this will be a beautiful photograph," he said, looking through the viewfinder. "Okay, do not move."

He pressed his finger down on the shutter button of the old camera, triggering the mechanisms within the lens to open momentarily and allow the light reflecting off the subjects to project inward toward the layers of chemicals on the face of the filmstrip, the light staining them.

He brought the camera down, looking at her.

"Will it turn out?" she asked.

"We will know later," he said, "when I have processed the film."

"Doesn't that stress you out? Not knowing if your images are going to look how you wanted them to? Not knowing if they're clear or totally out of focus?"

He looked at his camera.

"Like all good things," he said, "they take time."

She appreciated his calm, patient prose poems, each one a testament to the Italian spirit but confirmation for her of the supremacy of the American work ethic.

Does Italy even have a GDP? she damn near wondered.

He brought his face back up from his camera.

"Okay, may I introduce you to Roma now?" he asked.

"I appreciate the offer," she replied. "But, no, thank you. I need to follow through with the list I have compiled. I'm here to relax and experience Rome. The list will be how I do that."

He sighed in disappointment.

"What is next on your list?" he asked.

"The Appian Way Park."

"The *Parco dell'Appia Antica?*" he stated, surprised, but delighted by her answer. "This is an unusual first stop. Why is this so high on your list?"

"First, I'm obsessed with the Appian Way. It was a logistical miracle of the ancient world," she said. "Second, I scheduled the less popular items within the hours of peak visitation. Although it's slightly out of the way, I'll make up all that time and more by not standing in the lines of the highly-trafficked destinations just after lunch."

"You really have thought of everything. Incredible."

"That's what I do," she replied.

"Okay. Then let us go to the Appian Way," he said, standing up and putting his camera back on his shoulder.

Laughing, she asked, "What do you mean, *us?*"

"I have a Vespa. I will take you there. Think about it, you might even make up for the time you have lost due to the bus arriving late."

"You're okay adhering to my list?"

"I will accompany you to the park," he replied. "I have always liked it there. When we have finished with *La Via Appia* and you have had enough of me, I will leave you to your itinerary."

"As long as you stick to my list, you can join me for as long as you'd like."

As long as you'd like? she thought. *Shit.*

Normally, she would never have agreed to let a stranger join her for the day while traveling in a foreign city, or even while at home in the United States for that matter. But she liked that he had been kind to her, that he'd helped her with the two waiters, and she still felt bad that she'd become so defensive when he recognized she was U.S. military.

She closed her notebook and then paused, looking at the cover. After a deep breath, she placed it in a pocket of her weekender bag.

When in Rome, she thought.

They got up from the table as she left some cash with her bill.

"Your Vespa isn't red, is it?" she asked him.

"It is a beautiful red. Like the color of fully ripened apples when they are ready to be picked from the trees in the orchard."

"Of course it is," she said. "Alright. Let's do this."

The two of them walked across the street and got onto his Vespa. She was hesitant at first to sit so close behind him, but when he took off and began racing through the narrow, cobblestone streets, she scooted closer to him and grabbed his stomach with one of her hands, the other hand holding the weekender bag she'd secured to her body.

Federico took a right past a small bakery with a striped, red-and-white awning and then a quick left into a roundabout that surrounded a fountain, its bulbous, water-jet streams engulfing four bronze nymphs. Araceli was struck by the diversity of architecture she witnessed within such short distances. As Federico exited the roundabout and turned onto a main road, Araceli was not only presented with a display of symmetrical and opulently colorful hotels and museums, but colonnaded, white, stone buildings like the one she'd just departed from. Cheap, tin stands lined the streets, offering books, fruits, and antiques. And there were buildings that Araceli knew had to be much, much older than anything she'd seen before, their domes in various states of disrepair and their ancient, brown stucco crumbling off restored walls.

What kind of city planning does it take to keep a zoo like this running smoothly? she thought.

The two of them passed in front of one of the national museums. A line extended down a long sidewalk abutting a garden and nearly stretched all the way to the street.

Federico looked back at her over his shoulder.

"You would be in a line like that if you were not such a good planner," he said loudly over the noise of the street and the Vespa. "Maybe your methods do have *some* advantages."

After several minutes of zipping in and around the traffic of downtown Rome, Federico turned left past a busy street and into a tunnel beneath a train track. The tunnel was short, but it was dark and damp and overgrown with much foliage. The noises of the city faded behind them. Beyond the tunnel, a stone wall emerged beside the road, and Araceli could see that some kind of park or forest sat on the other side.

Federico pointed down to the road as he drove.

"You are now riding on the Appian Way," he said to her.

She looked down and was pleased to see how the stones neatly fit together, like a puzzle, just as she'd read. Although she realized these weren't the stones laid by the ancient Romans—only short sections preserve the original stones—she didn't care. That's not what interested her. She wasn't so much concerned with the engineering or the design of the Appian Way, but, rather, why it was created and how the Roman Republic, and later the Empire, used it. Regardless, the fitted stones stood out to her, and she enjoyed the sight of them.

Federico pulled into a small, gravel parking tract next to the stone wall and a shop that rented bicycles.

It was a quiet area, but there was more traffic (both vehicle and foot) than Araceli had expected. Of the many Romans there, some walked their dogs, some savored espressos, and some simply enjoyed an afternoon in the sun.

"You can leave your bag with the shop while we ride," Federico said to her as they approached the attendant.

"I'd rather keep it with me."

"While you ride a bicycle?"

"I'll be fine," she replied confidently, slightly playful.

"As you wish."

After each of them had rented bikes, they began their trip down the Appian Way, the stone wall on their left. Neither spoke for a little over one minute, until, sensing that Federico was nervous, Araceli broke the awkward silence.

"*Sustinendum Victoriam*," she stated proudly, looking over at Federico as the two rode side by side.

"What was that?" he asked. "Have you read that on one of the gravestones along the path?"

"No," she replied, laughing. "That's our motto. The motto of the Logistics Corps."

"Ahh, this is your motto. Sustaining Victory," he replied. "This makes a lot of sense."

"You know your Latin well."

"Every Italian knows a little Latin," he said.

"Who knows?" she continued. "Maybe those were the very words on the lips of the Roman senators when they commissioned the project. Or maybe the workers said it to themselves as they drew up the plans and laid these stones in the ground. *Sustinendum Victoriam.*"

"Why do you say this?"

"Do you know why this road was built?" she asked, the two looking to their left as they rode past a small and narrow, multi-story church constructed of marble, some blocks white, some yellow.

"I cannot say I do," he admitted. "But I do know it originally came to an end in Capua, very close to where I grew up, outside of Napoli."

"That's right. And it ended in Capua for a reason."

"Give me the history lesson," he said happily.

"When the Roman Republic was starting to expand their rule over the south of the peninsula, they ran into an independent, militaristic group called the Samnites. And they ran into them near Capua."

"Right, *le guerre sannitiche.* This rings a bell."

"In English, we call them the Samnite Wars."

"The Samnite Wars," he repeated jokingly, with as thick of an American accent as he could muster.

She laughed at his mockery as they stopped their bikes, coming to a fork in the road. There was a burnt orange tower where the roads split, a long row of hedges running parallel to the one on the right.

"Which way?" she asked.

"This way?" he said, holding a finger toward the road on the left.

"Was that a question or a statement?"

"I am almost certain this is the continuation of *La Via Appia*. The other road leads to some catacombs," he replied as they got back on their seats and started peddling again. "So, the Samnite Wars?"

"Yeah, to understand why the road was built, you need to understand the first half of the Second Samnite War was a disaster for the Romans. I mean, an utter disaster."

"For the Roman people or for their politicians' ambitions?" he prodded with a smirk.

Araceli grinned.

"They were a republic at this point, Federico," she replied. "Of the people, by the people, remember?"

Federico smiled.

"Go on," he said.

"The Romans weren't able to maintain a steady flow of personnel and equipment to the warfront, despite it being only a short distance away. The Samnites were in their home territory. The city of Rome was on the other side of a nasty marsh, or at least it was a nasty marsh back then. Without a good support network between Rome and the frontline, the Roman soldiers were left largely unequipped, and they lost a consequential battle."

"But if I remember correctly, this is not the end of the story," he said.

"Not even close," she replied. "Rome was not going to lose to the Samnites. They'd already colonized two towns near Capua, giving them a launchpad from which they could quickly attack their new adversaries, but access between Rome and the colonies was not easy."

"And here is where the Appian Way factors in?"

"A colony becomes insignificant if it's cut off and isolated," she said with a tone that communicated her expertise. "The Appian Way prevented that. When the second half of the war finally began, Rome was able to surge soldiers and equipment straight to the combat. *Sustinendum Victoriam.*"

"This was a faithful telling of the story, at least historically speaking," Federico concluded.

"I thought you said you weren't familiar with the Samnites?" Araceli responded, slightly flustered and confused. "Why did you ask me to give you the lesson?"

"I wanted to hear you say it. And, as I suspected, it was like the speech was delivered by an official mouthpiece of the empire."

"Again, they weren't yet an empire," she replied.

"That is what they always say."

She paused, trying to determine what he meant by the comment.

"What do you mean, *they*?" she started.

He looked at her knowingly.

"They didn't need to invade Capua, you know. They didn't need to invade *anywhere*. They chose to do those things," he said in a tone he hoped would keep the conversation on the lighter side.

"If it wasn't Rome, it would have been someone else," she replied, reaching for her belt loop. "That's just the way the world worked. Survival of the fittest empire."

There was no response from Federico. He simply stared straight ahead as they cycled down the old, stone road.

"You are right," he eventually admitted.

She wasn't convinced. She thought she might have pushed one of his buttons or brought up a subject he was sensitive to, but before she had the chance to try to salvage the conversation, he lightened the mood himself.

"And it all started here on the Appian Way," he said, turning to her with a solemn smile. "The beginning of Rome's long road to success."

His tone had become upbeat again, and Araceli was happy to see him smiling, hoping she hadn't offended him with her endorsement of some of Rome's more *imperial* tendencies.

She looked up at a stone arch over a path that led away from the road. There were many such paths. That section of the Appian Way was full of different offshoots and trails leading to catacombs, churches, and archaeological ruins spanning two millennia.

"It all started here," she repeated.

"You and the ancients, sustaining your victories across the known world," Federico said, looking at her out of the corner of his eye.

She turned her head at him; he looked down.

"I imagine the job looks a little different now than it did when the Romans were doing it," he quipped, continuing his point in a more playful way.

"The equipment has changed," she responded. "But the principles haven't."

"Explain."

"For example," she continued, "our creed says: 'I anticipate the warfighter's need for sustainment in all situations, at all times, under all conditions.'"

Federico glanced at her and nodded.

"Under all conditions," he said. "Like a malaria-ridden marsh."

"Especially a malaria-ridden marsh," she replied.

"It is a beautiful creed," he said.

"And that was only one line."

The road had become tight, and a steady stream of bicyclists came toward them from the opposite direction. Federico and Araceli were wedged close together. The closeness of their two bicycles allowed them to speak softy to one another, making their journey down the Appian Way feel intimate, familiar.

"I understand what you mean about the job looking different but the goal staying the same," Federico started. "We have new toys, but you cannot ask a hungry soldier to fight your wars. You must still move food from one place to another. And guns. And bullets."

"That's exactly right."

"You are very proud of your work," he said, just before he looked her directly in the eyes. "It is beautiful to see up close. When people are passionate about what they do."

She smiled and then quickly looked away.

"My mother was also passionate about what she did," he continued.

"For the American base in Naples?"

"Yes, for the Americans. The whole family was proud of her, especially my grandfather. She was only twenty years old when she started working there."

"How long did she work on base?" she asked.

"Look," Federico said, slowing down his bicycle and coming to a stop.

There was a long, unpaved driveway that extended from the Appian Way on their right, with one square column on each side of the driveway's entrance. Cypress trees lined the dirt road all the way down to a small villa at the end, its front staircase crowded with a group of people throwing rice into the air and cheering.

"A wedding," Federico said to Araceli.

The two watched as the bride and groom emerged through the front doors and walked down the staircase to great applause from their friends and families.

"It's beautiful," Araceli said under her breath.

"It is, really," he replied, turning his face from the wedding celebration to Araceli. "What is next on your list? How long do you intend to take the Appian Way, and when must I depart from you?"

"Well," she lingered, "the next item on my list is an early dinner and a bottle of red wine at a little, family-run osteria just off the Appian Way, near the end of the park."

They looked at each other, unblinking, until, after glancing down, Araceli asked, "Would you like to join me for the meal?"

"Araceli, I would love nothing more."

They looked back at the wedding celebration at the end of the driveway. The bride and groom had now fully descended the stairs and were giving hugs to the people congregated at the bottom.

"That bottle of red wine is calling," Federico said. "We will have a race. *Andiamo!*"

"Not fair!" she screamed as she got back onto her bicycle and started chasing after him. "I have this giant-ass bag on my back!"

Already several meters ahead of her, he looked back over his shoulder.

"That is your own fault!" he called out.

She scrunched her nose and gritted her teeth. A determined smile appeared across her face as she moved the bag to a more stable and streamlined position and kept peddling as hard as she could.

As the pair rounded a gradual turn and left the villa behind them, the arches and offshoots became increasingly less frequent and the stone wall receded, revealing open fields dotted with farmhouses and crumbling ruins.

Although she was in better shape than Federico, the bag and the distance lost to a late start presented significant obstacles, but as Federico slowly became larger in her view, Araceli's confidence that she might actually win grew.

Circular restaurant tables just off the edge of the road appeared in the distance.

That's gotta be it, she thought.

She passed Federico on her right, making a point not to make eye contact with him.

"*Mannaggia!*" he shouted. "Your bike has gears that mine does not!"

Now several meters ahead, she turned her face to him with a smirk and a wink.

"You really thought you could beat a soldier?" she said with a laugh before again facing forward on her bicycle.

Certain of her victory, she began to relax, but just before she was about to turn the corner into the courtyard area of the restaurant, she slammed on her brakes and jumped off the bike.

"The original stones!" she exclaimed.

Federico had to swerve to avoid her. After he came to an abrupt stop and collected himself, he put out the kickstand and walked to Araceli. They both panted, out of breath, as they stood across from each other, staring at the ground.

"These are some very nice stones," Federico said, looking for a way to seem even half as interested as Araceli looked to be.

Araceli bent down and placed her hand on one of the stones, laughing as she did so.

"I didn't think I'd care so much about a bunch of old rocks in the ground," she said. "But being here and touching this road, hand-built by the Romans…, it's… something."

She turned back to Federico and stood up. He didn't share her enthusiasm for the original stones, but he did like seeing her happy, and it showed on his smiling face.

"What a location for a restaurant!" she continued. "I love it already. Let's eat!"

Taking hold of their bicycles, the two walked through the open gate and saw stone replicas of ancient Roman statues and dining tables dispersed among a sprawling garden of wildflowers.

"*Siete qua per mangiare?*" asked an older man who was standing by himself among the statues.

He wore a dark blue, loose button-down shirt with sunglasses. Though his apparel set him apart from the statues, he'd been standing so still that Araceli and Federico hadn't noticed his presence at first.

"*Sì,*" said Federico, responding to the man's question of whether or not they were here to eat.

The man slowly shook his head at the two of them, saying that the kitchen was now closed and wouldn't be serving again until dinner.

Araceli gasped.

"See!" she exclaimed. "This is why you follow lists!"

Federico's cheeks became flushed. He was visibly embarrassed and avoided looking at Araceli while he considered what options he could take to get Araceli her meal.

Hearing Araceli speak English, the man walked toward them.

"Where do you come from?" he asked as he approached.

"I'm from the States," Araceli replied. "Well, I'm originally from Mexico, but I live in Italy now. It's a long story. Today, I've come from the bus station."

Federico and the man, who had now taken off his sunglasses, shared cordial glances as Araceli tried to navigate the response of her complicated origins.

As she finished, the man raised his wrist and studied his watch.

"Tell Paolo that Massimo sent you," he said in a conciliatory tone.

"Tell what to whom?" asked Araceli.

"Paolo," the man responded as he pointed down the small, side road toward the restaurant. "Tell him that I, Massimo, said you could eat."

Araceli and Federico thanked the man generously. As they strolled down the road, Federico whispered, "In Rome, you should always leave room for spontaneity," in her ear.

Walking into the courtyard, they found a massive olive tree emerging from the cobblestones. A stone tower with a wide, circular base loomed tall above the tables from the other side of the Appian Way. The restaurant, quaint and small, was built from the remnants of an old, agricultural villa, though it had been heavily renovated. Several diners lingered at tables in the courtyard, but they had long since finished eating and were now either sipping afternoon espressos or simply sitting in the sun, practicing the virtue of silence.

"*Scusa*," said a mustachioed man in a pressed, white shirt, who bore a striking resemblance to Massimo. "*La cucina è chiusa.*"

He was carrying a load of dishes into the restaurant from the tables in the courtyard.

Federico approached him, respectfully, and explained that Massimo had instructed them to tell a certain Paolo that they were welcome to eat.

The man sighed and peeked at his watch over the stack of dishes in his arms.

"My father is always promising the moon!" he said cordially but with a slightly exasperated flair. "Very well. Choose any table you'd like. Any table that is clean."

The two found a table near the olive tree, and Paolo promptly arrived with multiple plates of food he told them were leftovers from the lunch menu. He set down the plates and explained each in order. There was a serving of bruschetta with basil and honey, a plate of seasoned and fried sardines, and, finally, a basket of fresh, warm bread with a sauce made of garlic, butter, *pecorino romano* cheese, and several secret ingredients.

"I made it myself," Paolo stated proudly as Araceli dipped a piece of bread in the sauce, hardly containing how delicious she found it.

"I will return to take your orders shortly," Paolo said.

"He has kind eyes," Federico remarked when their server had entered the restaurant.

"Just like the old man's, only a generation younger," said Araceli, who was quite giddy, though doing her best not to show it.

As Federico walked her through the menu and its many dishes specific to the area, she daydreamed of a one-bedroom apartment in downtown Rome and a work assignment to study ancient logistics methodologies for the U.S. Army. Every morning she'd walk to her favorite riverside café on the way to the library, and on the weekends she'd offer tours of the Appian Way to visitors interested in the military history of the old road. She would spend her evenings with wine and books, or maybe she'd spend them with—

"Araceli?" Federico asked, interrupting her thoughts. "Araceli?"

She blinked and looked up from the menu.

"Yes?"

"Paolo is here. Are you ready to order?"

"Oh, yes! I'm sorry," she said, turning toward the waiter. "*Posso avere il pollo oxizomum? Grazie.*"

"*Va bene,*" Paolo responded with a smile. "I am known for this dish, ma'am. In fact, I've recently been informed that *The New York Times* will be including my own spin on *pollo oxizomum* in a piece on the gems of genuine Italian cuisine."

"That's lovely," Araceli responded in earnest.

Federico was less impressed. He didn't like the idea that *The New York Times* got to decide what constituted genuine Italian food, but he kept his thoughts to himself.

"I suspect you will enjoy it," Paolo said before picking the empty bruschetta plate off the table and heading back inside.

"Aren't you getting anything?" she asked Federico.

"Araceli," he said, laughing, "I have already ordered. You were here, but you were not here. For a few moments, I think you were inside your head."

"I'm sorry," she replied. "I was thinking about work."

"You were thinking about your work while smiling and staring at the menu?"

"Well, you do know how much I love work."

He squinted his eyes in her direction as if to communicate he was catching on to her and her secrets.

"Roma has intoxicated you, now, has it?"

"It's a beautiful city," she conceded. "It has a draw."

"I must admit something to you," Federico began, cracking one of the crisp breadsticks that had been set on the table. "Your strategy has proven very effective. A light snack with an espresso, a slow bicycle ride down the Appian Way, and now lunch at this lovely, little restaurant. Not too many sights, just the right amount. Relaxed and easy. The list was not nearly as burdensome as I imagined it to be. Well done."

"If we're admitting things to each other," she said, "then I should admit something to you."

"Please," he responded, "I am all ears, as you Americans say."

"We've already missed around half the items I'd scheduled to this point."

"What? I thought we were going to follow your list! The most important of all lists! What happened?"

"That was the plan!" she stated. "But when we started biking down the road and passing all the beautiful monuments, I realized I couldn't leave. I was compelled to keep peddling down the road, always just a little further, until I eventually realized my plan was ruined."

"We have strayed from your itinerary significantly."

"Yes, we have. I'd originally only allotted about ten minutes to the Appian Way. I wanted to visit the area, maybe take a quick photo, and then rush off to item number three."

"Which was?"

"The Catacombs of Domitilla. This restaurant was actually item six."

"Wow!" he said through a grin. "Then Roma really has gotten to you! You could not even get through the second destination without abandoning your schedule."

"I don't know what it is. The ruins everywhere, the pace at which people live their lives, the color of the sun.... I can't put my finger on it," she went on. "But the sun really does shine *differently* here."

"Yes, the sun in Roma is very special," Federico replied. "Oh, and I do not think you heard, but I have secured for us a tasty red wine. A *Cesanese* by *Corte Dei Papi San Magno*, grown in the hills south of the city. It has an earthy, wood-like taste. I think you will enjoy it, especially with the chicken that you ordered."

"Looking forward to it," she said.

"The grape that *Cesanese* wines are made from is very old and is typical of this region, so it is likely that the ancient Romans drank something similar to it."

She smiled.

"This is why I ordered it for us," he told her. "I thought you would enjoy the idea of drinking the same wine as your logistical ancestors, next to the road by which they became masters of their profession."

She could not help but display another smile. And this was a large, genuine smile, and, once again, Federico found that he loved seeing her happy.

Paolo approached their table, holding a bottle and two wine glasses. He brought the bottle toward Federico and showed him the label, receiving a nod and a, *"perfetto, grazie."* Paolo then poured a small amount of wine into one glass and handed it to Federico, who, after carefully accepting the glass, brought it to the table and moved it in a circle. Lifting it to his face and then holding it toward the sky, he inspected the wine for debris, and then, just before bringing it to his mouth, he stopped.

"No," he said, looking at Araceli. "You inspect the wine. If you like it, we will drink it. If not, we choose another."

"I don't really know what to taste for," she replied. "I love wine, but I'm not a connoisseur or anything."

"It is not as difficult as it seems. Do not be fooled by the pretense. Just make sure the wine is not too much of any one thing: bitter, fruity, woody. Even a cheap wine should not overpower any one aspect of your palette. You only need to ensure the wine is balanced and has not gone bad in the cellar."

"If you say so," she said, accepting the glass from Federico and bringing it to her mouth for a sip.

Both Paolo and Federico looked to her as she savored the bit of wine and tried to identity whether any one flavor was too overbearing.

"I think it's great," she said. "We'll take it."

"*Bene,*" Paolo replied as he poured two glasses and set the rest of the bottle on the table between them.

Federico picked up his glass and raised it to Araceli.

"To new friends and *la bella vita di Roma,*" he said. "I have enjoyed spending the afternoon with you, Araceli. Thank you for letting me join you. *Salute.*"

"*Salute,*" she responded, clinking her glass against his and taking a sip.

"Why did you walk over to my table in the first place?" she asked after setting down the glass. "Earlier today, why did you help me sort out the cat meat situation?"

He laughed under his breath and set down the glass, looking up at her with a sweet, relaxed expression.

"When I watched you walk across the street, I had a feeling that you were American military," he said. "There was something about the way you walked that struck me as... familiar. And then when I heard you talking with the waiter, I was almost sure of it. As I watched you, I was reminded of my childhood."

"I reminded you of your childhood?"

"It is difficult to explain," he replied. "I have such wonderful memories of my youth, surrounded by Americans at my grandfather's shop, at home in my mother's small apartment.... You brought those memories back to me, and, after that, I had to talk with you. I was so curious about who you were, why you were here."

She could hear the authenticity in his voice, and his answer made her happy, but while this spotlight was on her, she felt shy and didn't know how to navigate the feeling. She took a drink of wine.

"Why were there so many Americans at your grandfather's shop?" she asked after the sip. "What did he do for a living?"

"My grandfather was a butcher," Federico answered fondly. "He owned a meat shop. He was a small, confident man. Every morning, he would begin his day with a freshly cleaned, white apron, and, by the end of the day, it was always, always covered in bright red blood from top to bottom. I remember playing a game where I would look for his bloody handprints on his apron, and then, when I found them, I would excitedly point them out."

Araceli smiled, seeing him recollect memories of his grandfather.

"Americans do love their meat," she said.

"Yes, they do. But this is not the reason his shop was so popular with the American military in Napoli."

"What *was* the reason?" she asked.

"When my mother started working on base, it was a very intense time with the Soviets. They had been placing missiles near their border with Western Europe, and, in response, the United States planned to place their own missiles in Europe to make the Soviets stop what they were doing."

"When was this?" she asked. "Late 70's, early 80's?"

"Yes," Federico replied. "My mother began working on base in 1980. By that point, my grandfather had become a fierce defender of the American presence in Europe. Whenever someone new came into his shop, he would tell them his daughter worked on the American base and she was helping to save Italy from the communists!"

He paused, smiling as he thought of his grandfather.

"It is not like she was decoding Soviet secrets or anything," he continued. "She was a cook. But that did not matter. To my family, my mother's work was important."

Paolo arrived at their table with both plates of food and asked how they were enjoying the wine. Federico told him it was exactly what they had wanted.

"Your family sound like nice people," Araceli said after the waiter left and they took their first bites.

Federico nodded his head, his mouth full of food.

"So, go on," she continued. "How did your grandfather's shop come to be overrun by Americans?"

"That first year my mother worked on base, things began to heat up in Italy. People were suspicious of their political opponents. If a communist came into my grandfather's shop, he would kick them out, telling them he did not want Soviet spies lurking around his family. As you can imagine, the shop began to have a reputation, especially with the Americans. Every day, more and more Americans would come into his shop to buy their meat. My grandfather quickly became friends with many of them, and his fame among the American military in Napoli spread."

"Sounds like it worked out pretty well for him," she said.

"That is not even half the story," he responded. "Of course, I was not even born yet, but I have heard this story over and over growing up. Maybe more than one thousand times!"

Araceli laughed, as did Federico.

"How is your food?" she asked.

"Paolo must have made some changes to the classic recipe. The sauce is *different*. And how is your oxizomum?"

"You were right," she replied. "The wine pairs nicely with the chicken. I've never had anything like it. Is this cream some kind of a fish sauce?"

"That is precisely what it is. It is called *garum*. A fermented delicacy of the ancient Romans. Archaeologists have even found some preserved at Pompeii. Today, it is sold all over Roma. I suspect Paolo has added his own touch to that, too."

"Seems that between the wine and the dish, this meal is authentically ancient," she said. "But, please, finish telling me about your grandfather and his shop."

"Right," he started. "After he had become the most famous meat supplier of the American military in Napoli, something very bad happened in Italy. One of your American generals was abducted by an Italian communist group. The man was taken right from his apartment in the center of Verona."

"General Dozier," Araceli responded. "Taken by the Red Brigades and held hostage for over a month."

"You are familiar with this abduction?"

"Anyone who lives off-post is required to take a class about what happened to the general and how to make sure it doesn't happen to us."

"If you have taken this class, why did you decide to get on the Vespa of the first stranger you met in Roma? Could I not be trying to abduct you right now?"

"Dozier's kidnappers dressed like plumbers or electricians or something. Blue-collar, working men who pulled a gun on his wife while they stuffed the general in a car," she said with the faintest beginning of a playful smile. "They weren't dressed as Bohemian layabouts with nice hair, taking film photos of Rome's stray cats. Too on the nose for a radical communist."

"With nice hair?" Federico repeated back to her.

Araceli smiled.

"It's crazy they actually pulled it off," she replied, changing the subject away from her opinion of his hair. "They actually got him. Just a bunch of students."

"He embodied NATO here, and many Italians believed he was going to be killed," he replied. "Only a few years earlier, the *Brigate Rosse* had abducted one of our former prime ministers. His name was Aldo Moro. While they kept him in captivity, they put him on trial and then killed the man!"

"I've never heard of Moro," she said sadly. "How terrible."

"Yes, the *Brigate Rosse* was a dangerous faction. Deep connections to groups in the Eastern Bloc, so when these guerrillas took your general, many feared the worst."

"Well, many thanks to you Italians for rescuing him," Araceli added.

"Sometimes we find the time for more than having nice hair and taking pictures of cats."

She smiled.

"And after the incident," Federico continued, "American military working in Italy became extremely cautious about where they went, who they spent time with, from which store they bought groceries, everything."

"I'm starting to put the pieces together," she said. "I'm guessing your grandfather's shop became even more popular with the Americans?"

"He could not keep up with the demand! He opened a second shop, even closer to base than the first. The Americans turned my grandfather from a struggling shop owner to the richest butcher in Napoli. When I was old enough, I started working for him. I even ran one of the shops for a while."

"That's quite the story," Araceli said, nodding her head. "Did your mother ever leave her job on base and help you and your grandfather with the business?"

"No, my mother never did. She kept her job on base for more than thirty years. From Tuesday to Saturday, she staffed a cafeteria, never taking different work, never traveling, never getting married, and then, just a few years ago, she died of cancer."

"I'm sorry to hear that," she said. "And your father?"

"I did not have a father."

"You didn't have a father?" she asked.

"I did not."

"Was he... an American?" she inquired, tentatively. "Who didn't stay in Italy when his tour was over?"

Really? Why did I ask that? she thought.

"My father could not have been an American because I did not have one. I had a mother. And I had a grandfather. And they were the ones who raised me. The only people who raised me."

She smiled at him, softly, watching him finish the glass of wine and then following suit. She figured his father must have been an American, who, for some reason or another, abandoned him and his mother when it was time to transfer duty stations. She had heard of many similar stories playing out across the military community in Vicenza, where she was stationed. She'd even heard a story recently in which an American soldier carried on a relationship with an Italian girl for two full years. When it came time for him to leave Italy, the girl assumed he would marry her and bring her with him. Instead, he confessed that he was already married and that his wife and family were waiting for him back home in the United States.

Araceli felt sorry for Federico. She wished she could comfort him, but she didn't want to push further. She now understood why it was so easy for him to recognize her and why he must have been drawn to her to begin with. Three generations of this man's heritage had the course of their lives drastically altered by the U.S. presence in Italy, and Federico himself, a boy born to a deserted mother, was a byproduct of that presence.

"Araceli," Federico said, pouring two more glasses of wine for them, "I have an idea."

"Okay?"

"You have already destroyed your plan for the day, yes? And there can be no salvaging of the itinerary, yes?"

"I would need to put some serious work into that itinerary to even come close to salvaging it," she said. "And, honestly, I don't feel like doing that right now. You were right, Federico. Rome is meant to be savored, not rushed."

He smiled back at her, looking very pleased at what she'd said.

"And I'm not even stressed about it," she continued with a smile and a lighthearted tone. "Which is weird for me."

He slammed his fist down on the table between them, as if to communicate that what he was about to say was of the utmost importance.

"In this case," he started, "we must go and crash the wedding we passed earlier."

"I'm sorry?" she babbled. "I'm not going to a wedding I haven't been invited to!"

"Listen," he said. "The ceremony, the dinner, the toasts, they are over. All they have to do now is dance and drink. No one will even notice we are there."

"Federico, my Italian is not nearly good enough to *crash* a wedding," she said in a hushed voice, looking around to make sure no one was listening to them talk about crashing a wedding. "We'd be caught as soon as I opened my mouth."

"You do not need to speak to anyone. We walk in, have a drink and a dance, and leave. Easy as that."

"This is absurd. What would I even wear? I can't go in these clothes."

"Do you not have something nice in that bag you have been carrying around all day? Maybe a dress?"

"I guess I do have a dress in the bag…."

"It is settled!" he exclaimed.

"Just hold on a minute," she implored, still cautious of listeners who might be judging her.

"Araceli, it will be fun. Trust me."

"And what about you? What would you wear? You look like a...," she paused, tilting her head to the side. "Well, you look like a Federico who's been out in the sun, biking all day."

He turned, casually, in his seat. There was an older gentleman sitting in a corner of the courtyard. He had on a white shirt, like Federico, but also a tie. On the table in front of him sat a newspaper, which he'd been reading since the two of them arrived at the restaurant.

"We will make a deal," Federico said, turning back to Araceli. "We will leave it to fate. If I can convince the man in the corner to give me his tie, then we will crash the wedding. You will wear the dress, and I will tuck in this shirt. We will blend right in. If he does not give me the tie, we give up the idea."

She glanced over Federico's shoulder at the man in the corner with the tie and then looked back at Federico.

"Deal," she said, holding out her hand. "No chance that man will give you his tie."

"We will see," he stated as he stood up from the table.

She watched as Federico approached the man in the corner and introduced himself. Although she couldn't hear what they were saying, she could tell it was going well.

How is he already making him laugh? she thought.

Federico pointed to his shirt and then began tucking it into his khakis. The man stood up, slipped the tie above his head, and placed it around Federico's neck, tightening it for him.

Unbelievable, she thought. *That was fast....*

Federico thanked the man for his generosity and returned to the table, an elated grin across his face when he sat down.

"How did you do that?" Araceli probed. "That took you like ninety seconds, tops."

"I simply asked him politely," Federico replied with a shrug of the shoulders. "Apparently, he's a friend of Massimo."

"We're really doing this?" she asked, smiling broadly.

"You are in Rome, and we are crashing that wedding," he responded. "Go to the bathroom and change. I will pay the bill. When you return, we will ride our bicycles to the wedding."

"You don't need to pay the bill, Federico. We can split it."

"Please, I insist. It is the least I can do in return for imposing myself on you all day and ruining your itinerary."

She leaned in over the table.

"Thank you," she said. "That's very kind of you."

When Araceli came back from the bathroom, Federico was waiting next to the bikes, engaging in the kind of productive loitering men do when women visit restrooms, in this case making sure the tires weren't losing air. He watched her approach, very much taken by the way she looked in the lemon-colored sundress she'd changed into.

"Do you think this is dressy enough?" she asked.

"I think you look incredible."

Feeling the attention shift completely in her direction yet again, she looked down.

"Araceli," Federico continued, "may I take your bag while we ride to the wedding?"

"Sure," she responded with a smile as she lifted her face. "That would be nice."

When the two rode their bicycles out of the gate that surrounded the courtyard, they turned onto the Appian Way in the direction from which they'd come. Peddling slowly, they enjoyed the view and pointed out interesting monuments they'd missed during their race. The road was less crowded than it had been earlier, and although still warm, the temperature began to drop, and a light, summer breeze kicked up around them. Araceli couldn't believe she was about to trespass on a stranger's wedding, in a foreign country, with someone she just met. But the anxiety that would have normally surrounded a similar departure from her standard behavior was blunted by the novelty and thrill of the situation, and even more so by the many butterflies that were flying in circles around her stomach.

"At the wedding," Federico said, "do your best not to speak. If someone talks to you, I will distract them and change their focus."

"Whatever you say," she replied.

After they arrived at the road that led to the villa, they stashed their bicycles by one of the square columns in case they had to make a quick getaway. As they walked down the road, they saw a large, open-air tent beside the villa, with people dancing and partying inside. No one seemed to notice them despite Federico carrying Araceli's bag and looking slightly out of place because of it. The sun was already low in the sky, casting long shadows in front of the celebrants on the lawn and providing cover as the couple moved.

As they got closer to the center of the action, the property opened up to a meticulously groomed garden, replete with hedges, cypress trees, and fountains. Walking paths of white sand and pebbles wound their way though all of it. Araceli loved that string lights had been hung from the tent to large trees in the garden and the villa, creating what she believed to be one of the most beautiful wedding landscapes she'd ever seen.

Standing on her tiptoes, she placed her mouth directly against Federico's ear.

"I think we're underdressed for this place," she whispered.

Federico placed his index finger over his mouth and then took Araceli by the hand, leading her into the tent toward some tables in the corner. He placed her bag in one of the chairs, and they walked up to the bar, where Federico ordered two negroni cocktails.

Over the course of five or six songs, Federico and Araceli stayed on the side of the dance floor, enjoying the music and the lights while sipping slowly on their cocktails. They stood very close together, exchanging a series of flirtatious looks and gentle nudges. Araceli could feel the hair on her forearm stand up whenever it brushed against Federico.

The music had been mostly upbeat and Italian, but when Presley's "Can't Help Falling in Love" started to play, Federico took the nearly empty glass from Araceli's hand, set it on a table behind them, and pulled her onto the dance floor. He drew her close as the two swayed back and forth to the music. They were surrounded by other couples doing the same, including the bride and groom, toward the front of the tent, near the DJ.

His cheek touching her own, Federico leaned in closer and whispered in her ear, "Come back to Roma next weekend."

She moved her head back to look into his eyes. The DJ turned down the multi-colored lights for the slow song, and everything under the tent was dark. Placing her hand on the back of his neck and pulling his face toward her, she closed her eyes and kissed him on the lips.

He was surprised, but stayed cool.

"Is that a yes?" he whispered.

Araceli put her index finger over her mouth, mimicking what he'd done to her earlier, and then pulled his face toward her a second time, kissing him again.

"I like this method of communication," he said quietly.

She couldn't help but smile.

The song ended, and the multi-colored lights returned. Party music began to play, and everyone on the dance floor formed a large circle, inside of which one of the more outgoing guests of the wedding began dancing alone to the pulsing song. Around him, people clapped, swayed, and laughed.

After a little more than a minute, the solo dancer pointed at none other than Araceli, who tried to refuse the nomination by pantomime. But Roman crowds are demanding things, and when the party-goers began cheering for her to enter the dance circle, Federico put his hand on the small of her back and gave her a light push into the middle. Her right hand shot down toward her belt loop. When she discovered that she was wearing a dress and didn't have a belt loop to rely on, she simply grabbed a piece of the dress instead. As she did so, she turned back to Federico with the same expression he imagined Caesar to have gazed upon Brutus with at the moment of betrayal. Realizing there was no way out of it, Araceli accepted her fate and began moving her body to the music, completely terrified and altogether outside of her comfort zone. But at least she had that piece of dress on her right hip.

Enraptured by the grace with which she moved her hips, Federico reached for the camera that had been strapped over his neck and under his arm since arriving at the wedding. After adjusting the settings to the light, he took pictures of Araceli dancing in the circle, the real guests applauding around her.

To Federico, the moment couldn't have been more perfect. He thought she looked adorable, enticing, and alluring, flailing one of her arms (the other oddly restricted to her side) and trying not to be found out as an American. This was Roma. This was what he'd tried to convince Araceli of earlier that afternoon, that the most precious moments in life cannot be planned. He knew, deep in his soul, that he'd remember this night for the rest of his life.

When her turn was over, she dashed from the dance floor back to Federico's side, where she gave him a hug and punched him in the arm, nervously giggling all the way. After a few more people had taken their turn in the middle, the circle dissipated, and the dance floor returned to normal.

Araceli and Federico retreated to the table where he'd previously placed her bag. While she waited for him on the other side of the chairs, he took out the used roll of film and placed it inside her bag for safe keeping. When he looked up from zipping it shut, he saw a man in a black tuxedo approaching Araceli.

"*Chi Sei? Ti conosco?*" the man asked Araceli, who stalled and then looked to Federico as he rushed up to them from behind.

"*Ciao,*" Federico replied. "*No, non ci conosci. Siamo amici di tua moglie. Congratulazioni, comunque. Il matrimonio è stato bellissimo.*"

Upon hearing Federico's answer, the man looked at him with a puzzled expression, his eyebrows twisted. Araceli was certain their cover was blown.

"*Non sono lo sposo,*" the man said. "*Sono il testimone.*"

Federico's mouth dropped open, and, after a moment of panic, uttered the first thing that came to his mind, "*Mi dispiace. A volte mi confondo.*"

Araceli's eyes were wide as Federico turned toward her, pale.

"We—need—to—go," he silently mouthed, motioning his head toward the road.

"*Cos'hai detto?*" the man in the tuxedo inquired of Federico.

Araceli picked up her bag, and they hastened away from the table and out of the tent. As they hurried down the driveway toward the Appian Way, not so quickly as to draw even more attention to themselves, they heard the raised voice of the man in the black tuxedo shouting to the actual groom that the wedding had been infiltrated. At this, they took off in a sprint. Just before reaching their bikes, they turned around and saw that a large group of people had gathered at the edge of the tent and were watching them get away.

Araceli raised her hand in the air to wave goodbye, shouting, "*Mi dispiace! Ma grazie mille!*"

"Hurry, hurry," Federico urged as the two mounted their bikes and started peddling.

Once a safe distance from the villa and sure they weren't being chased, they looked at each other and simultaneously erupted in laughter.

"How crazy was that?" Federico asked. "Are you glad you listened to me? We will carry this story with us forever."

"I have to say," Araceli replied, laughing so hard she was nearly out of breath, "I can't remember the last time I had this much fun."

"I might have taken some of the best photographs of my life this evening. I cannot wait to develop the roll. They will be dark, grainy, and probably out of focus, but I am telling you, these photos will be special."

There was almost nobody on the road at that point, but the two still rode their bicycles very close together back to the rental shop and Federico's Vespa. They peddled slowly, catching their breath and enjoying the night air. There were not many lights, and the darkness made the road and the ruins look far different than they'd looked under a bright sun.

"Let me get this straight," Araceli said. "That guy asked us who we were, and you told him we were friends of the bride."

"Right."

"And then you congratulated him on getting married, but he told you he didn't get married and that he was actually the best man?"

"Exactly," Federico said, starting to laugh again.

"Unbelievable! There were probably only two men there wearing a tux like that. Of course you congratulated the one who *didn't* just get married."

"A beautiful ending to our night at a stranger's wedding," he said. "I would not have wanted us to leave any other way."

Araceli became quiet, prompting Federico to ask if everything was alright and if she was feeling okay.

"There's something I've been meaning to tell you," she replied. "I should have said this back at the restaurant, but I didn't because I was shy. It's been on my mind since."

"What is it?"

"I'm sorry you never knew your father. Must have been difficult for you growing up, not having him around or even knowing who he was."

Federico sighed and looked at her with a smile Araceli found sweet and endearing. But a moment later, his eyes became dim.

"These things happen," he responded. "Cases like mine are not unique."

"I know they happen," she said. "But it can't be *that* common."

He looked at her out of the corner of his eye.

"There are many of us, Araceli. Trust me."

A minute of silence passed, and Araceli considered the implications of his opinion.

"I'm sorry, then," she offered.

"I had it better than most. I am not trying to say I am some kind of Vietnamese *bui-dòi* or something. Those kids had it worse."

"Your situations are entirely different," Araceli responded. "That was war."

"Are our situations so different? Was I not left behind, too?"

Though Araceli understood where Federico was coming from, his tone and the comparison to kids born of soldiers in war-torn Vietnam made her uncomfortable.

"You make it sound like your mother didn't have a say in the matter."

"Did she choose my father? Sure. But she never expected to be abandoned," Federico said. "Are you defending the man's actions?"

"I'm not defending anyone, Federico," Araceli replied. "But it seems you and your family have made the best of it."

"We should not have had to," he shot back. "The United States should never have been here."

"You can't be serious," she said, her expression unamused. "We made sure communism didn't spread here. And we did damn fine job."

"And now?"

"And now, what?"

"And now the threat of communism has passed. Why are you still here?" he asked as his voice trailed off.

"You're right, Federico. It's not 1980 anymore, and the Soviet Union is gone. But radical Islam exists, and it's American blood and American money that keep Europe safe. And guess who else is knocking on Europe's door," she said as she stared at him with narrowed eyebrows. "Russia."

Federico stayed silent. He'd wished the conversation hadn't come up, but it had. And now he was invested.

"Nothing to say?" Araceli continued.

Federico turned his head to her; they locked eyes as they glided down the path, through the night.

"If the U.S. really cared about Russian expansion, they would have done something when Putin invaded Crimea. Last I checked, Crimea is in Europe. So you will need to forgive me for questioning the goals of NATO in the 21st century."

She scoffed, looking at him sharply as she shook her head. They had drifted farther apart as they cycled down the road and were no longer talking with the same softness or kindness as they had been only minutes earlier.

"What are you trying to say?" she asked after a pregnant pause in the conversation.

"I am trying to say that European security sounds like a great excuse for an empire that wants to use Europe as a staging ground for operations around the globe. You probably know a great deal about that, don't you, captain logistics?"

The last bit stung, and she couldn't believe what she was hearing. Looking straight ahead, she scolded herself for how stupid she was to let this man into her life, for developing feelings for him after only a day, for defiling her itinerary. She looked back in his direction.

"You sound like a petulant, spoiled, little kid," she said.

"And you sound like a naive girl who can speak about the Appian Way and the colonies it transported soldiers to, but cannot see that the U.S. uses Europe the same way the Romans used Capua."

"Don't follow me," she said as she started peddling her bike as hard and fast as she could, leaving Federico behind her.

"I am sorry, Araceli!" he called out to her. "I am sorry! I should not have said that!"

"Don't follow me!" she yelled back.

As soon as she turned the corner and escaped from view, he felt terrible. He wished, more than anything, that he could speak to her again, but, as she'd requested, he did not follow her. He was convinced it was only a matter of time before she'd turn around and come peddling back to him.

But she did not turn her bicycle around. She rode faster than she had during their race, all the way back to the bicycle shop, where she locked the bike to the designated rack. She saw Federico's Vespa sitting in the lot. Looking at it made her sick.

Walking briskly down the street toward the center of Rome, she called a taxi service and requested a driver come to her location. When the taxi driver picked her up, she told him the address of the rental she'd booked in preparation for the trip.

It wasn't a long drive. When they arrived at the address, the driver told her the fee. She reached into her bag to grab her wallet, but she pulled something else out instead. In her hand was the roll of film Federico had placed there after her excursion on the dance floor. All her best memories from the day came flooding back. At that moment, she wanted nothing more than to run into Federico's arms and kiss him like she did when they were listening to Elvis and holding each other close.

"Turn the car around," she said.

"What?"

"Please. I'll pay double. Just take me to the bicycle shop at the beginning of the Appian Way. And please, drive as fast as you can."

As the Romans

When We're Away

4:51 a.m.

Morning, girl!

8:44 a.m.

Hey baby
Sorry for the late reply
Just dropped the kids off at school

8:49 a.m.

I know…
It was a bit late

8:50 a.m.

Lindsey wouldn't come out of her room
All morning. I had to force my way in and bring her out myself
And Jack wouldn't stop taking his clothes off !

8:53 a.m.

When are you getting back again???
I'm sorry. Don't mean to stress you. It was just a rough morning with them

8:54 a.m.

How's your day going so far?

12:18 p.m.

> I'm sorry for all that
> I wish I was there to help!

12:19 p.m.

> Can I call you?

12:29 p.m.

> My lunch is almost over
> Need to start heading back to the range

12:30 p.m.

> Love you!

12:37 p.m.

SHIT!
Just seeing this
Any chance you can still talk??

12:39 p.m.

Well I guess not…
Can we talk tonight?
Love you!

12:43 p.m.

I wish you were here, too.
Just a bad morning with her. Again.

9:12 p.m.

Kids are down for the night
Call whenever you can

9:23 p.m.

*if you can…

11:42 p.m.

> Sorry
> Just getting done at the range
> Exhausted. Need to get some sleep
> Tell the kids I say good morning when they wake up

4:51 a.m.

> Morning you!

8:32 a.m.

Kids are dropped off!
Morning!

8:33 a.m.

We miss you so much

8:34 a.m.

Call whenever you have time today

12:48 p.m.

Not going to have time today
My team is working with the Slovenians in the glass house room clearing stuff
We only have the facility for one day so we'll be in there until lights out tonight

12:49 p.m.

Sorry! Love you!

12:53 p.m.

Okay
Tomorrow will be three weeks
It honestly feels like three months

12:56 p.m.

How do wives with kids make it through real deployments?
I know you're only a few hundred miles away
But you're not with us. You might as well be as far away as Iraq

1:14 p.m.

I know it's much better than Iraq…
I'm glad you're not there

1:19 p.m.

We just need you here…

9:49 p.m.

Hey
There's a surprise waiting for you in Telegram

11:55 p.m.

Well, I'm glad you warned me!
You almost made my team super jealous.
Close quarters in here.

11:58 p.m.

They don't care about me and my two baby body
I'm sure their ladies are sending them the same things
Only better

11:59 p.m.

Well Dylons and the Italian girl he was seeing just broke up
The other two are single
So, no
No one is waiting for them. Or sending them anything

12:01 a.m.

They couldn't even make it through their first rotation
Dylons and the Italian girl
Didn't see that coming
I thought they'd last a while

12:04 a.m.

They were heading in that direction
But I think the rotation was the last nail in the coffin

12:06 a.m.

You guys have been gone a long time!

12:07 a.m.

>It's only been three weeks!

12:08 a.m.

Easy for you to say!
You're not the one raising two kids by yourself

12:10 a.m.

>My soldiers are basically kids
>They need just as much supervision
>Trust me
>Lol

12:14 a.m.

Seriously though
Do you know when you guys are coming back to Italy yet?

12:16 a.m.

>There was talk about maybe coming back next Sunday
>But now its sounding like it might be a bit earlier

12:19 a.m.

Well that would be nice

12:20 a.m.

Rumor is that they want us to have three full weekends home
before we leave again for the big six week exercise in August

12:22 a.m.

Summer training schedule is so ducking brutal here
Can we please go back to Fort Bragg!

12:24 a.m.

One more summer
then we'll be off to our next duty station
Let's try to enjoy the rest of our time in Italy while we can

12:25 a.m.

You should take the kids to Venice this weekend!

12:26 a.m.

Lindsey has a soccer game
Hopefully I can convince her to play. This morning she said she wouldn't
And you know we don't like traveling without you

12:27 a.m.

Who are they playing?

12:29 a.m.

Ramstein
The girls teams from the base in Ramstein are spending the whole weekend down here in Italy
They'll be playing Aviano on Friday and us on Sunday

12:31 a.m.

Damn I wish I could be there

12:32 a.m.

I know
They don't get many games a year
It would be nice if you could be here for at least one…

12:33 a.m.

I know it would.
Tell Lindsey how much I wish I could watch her play

12:34 a.m.

You could tell her yourself if you made time to call

12:36 a.m.

> It's not that easy
> We're busy. All day, every day.
> By the time we're done the kids are in bed

12:37 a.m.

Yeah, I know
But she's missing you. And she's acting out. These rotations
aren't just hard for me and you
Try to find time in the next few days

12:39 a.m.

> **OUTGOING VOICE CALL**
> No answer

12:40 a.m.

> You know I miss them too
> How could I not
> And I miss you

12:41 a.m.

Late here.. Don't want to wake them

12:42 a.m.

>Okay

12:43 a.m.

I'll let you get to bed
I'm sure you need some sleep

12:44 a.m.

>Actually I can sleep in a bit in the morning.
>Maybe I can put that surprise to use if everyone's gone before I need to get up ;)

12:45 a.m.

Why can you sleep in?

12:46 a.m.

>I was chosen to be part of a small group of soldiers to visit a Slovenian school tomorrow
>For a show and tell kind of thing with the kids
>To win their hearts and minds lol

12:48 a.m.

Why did they choose you?

12:49 a.m.

The company commander recommended me to battalion
They were probably looking for soldiers with young kids

12:50 a.m.

Well that sounds like it will be fun

12:51 a.m.

It's a change of pace
It'll be nice

12:55 a.m.

Okay, well I am going to get to bed
Have fun tomorrow!
Love you

12:56 a.m.

Love you too!
Goodnight

***

Waking to his alarm at 7:45 a.m., Sergeant Robert Scheben sat up, totally alone in the 40-person tent; everyone else had long since woken, eaten, and departed for their various training missions and tasks. He hadn't had a proper haircut since the night before leaving for Slovenia. His recent field cut, as they called it, was the result of using clippers without a guard on all hair below the top of the ear. On another man, one might look at the hairstyle and assume the individual a monk, but on Scheben, there was no doubt. He was a soldier in the field. A soldier with stubborn, day-old face paint behind his ears, in his eyebrows, and on the back of his neck.

The olive drab cot he had slept on for the past three weeks creaked ferociously as he shifted his weight and lowered his feet to the sandy floor. He did *not* put the surprise to use. Instead, he proceeded to select his least-soiled socks and underwear from the stack of folded clothes sitting on the ground near the head of his cot. The uniform he put on was smudged with dried, crusted dirt in the knees and the elbows, but so by now were all six sets of uniforms he'd brought to Slovenia. After dry shaving and brushing his teeth, he left the tent and walked in the direction of the main entry and exit point to the training grounds. The morning fog had just begun to break with the rising temperature of a typical Slovenian summer day, and, as Scheben left the area, he found a black passenger van that was parked on the side of an unpaved road outside a chainlink fence that surrounded the military site.

"You Scheben?" called out a man through a drag of a cigarette, leaning against the driver's door of the van.

"Yeah," Scheben replied cautiously as he approached the man, who was wearing casual civilian clothes. "And you're Sergeant Marshal?"

"That's me."

"Good. Then I'm in the right place."

"That you are," Marshal said as he tossed his cigarette onto the sandy road and turned toward the van, knocking loudly against one of the windows. "Alright, everyone, pack it in. Time to pop smoke."

A door opened on the other side of the van, drawing Scheben's attention to a group of three entering the vehicle, two in uniform and one in a denim jacket. When he opened his side of the van's door to get in, he recognized a friend of his from a different company in the battalion.

"Schebs!" exclaimed his friend as the two saw each other through the middle of the van. "I didn't know you were coming along today."

"Neither did I, until last night," Scheben replied as he stepped up into the vehicle.

"Yeah, same here. I heard this trip was pretty last minute. Command must have been caught off guard when our return date got moved left."

"We're heading home early, then?"

"That's just what people are saying. Only a rumor," replied the friend, a sergeant named Elliot, as he clicked his seatbelt.

Scheben grunted.

"Scheben, you remember Specialist Tadros? I think you two have met once or twice," Elliot said as he gestured toward a young-looking soldier sitting next to him with hands folded politely in his lap and glasses resting neatly on his round, child-like face.

Scheben nodded in his direction.

"Good morning, sergeant," Tadros said respectfully as he looked at Scheben.

The van took off down the road, kicking up dust behind it. Scheben turned his head to glance at the third individual, who had taken a seat in the back, in the row of open seats behind Scheben, Elliot, and Tadros.

"Who's the dude in civies?" Scheben asked under his breath, leaning toward his friend.

"That's the photography guy from brigade public affairs," Elliot enthusiastically answered.

"Brigade?" Scheben asked.

"You know you're about to do some cool shit when brigade sends someone down," Elliot said quietly, slightly tongue in cheek.

Scheben turned again to face the photographer.

"I thought I recognized you," he said. "I follow you on Instagram."

"Oh yeah? Thank you very much."

"You look clean, man. No chance you haven't showered in three weeks. You just get here?"

"Yeah," the photographer responded. "We got in a couple days ago. Only shooting part of this one. I'm leaving for another exercise in Spain the day after tomorrow."

Scheben raised an eyebrow and looked at Elliot.

"Damn. How do I get his job?" he asked sarcastically.

"And give up the infantry? You'd come crawling back in two seconds. Guys like us are masochists. If we weren't getting rained on, yelled at, or sleeping in the dirt, we'd be paying Romanian strippers to tie us down and whip us."

The photographer laughed from the back seat.

"I don't know," Scheben said. "I think I could give it up, man."

"Like hell, you could," Elliot countered. "Just think about how much money we're saving. A Romanian dominatrix will drain your bank account faster than a divorced wife with four of your own kids."

Scheben stared at Elliot with a blank, slightly questioning expression.

"What, you have a better plan?" Elliot asked.

"Is there anything you won't say?"

"Nope. Lost the filter in airborne school. Took a major concussion on the last jump. Still graduated, though. Never been the same since."

The car fell silent as they tried to gather whether or not Elliot was joking.

"I didn't know that, man," Scheben started slowly. "I'm sorry to hear that."

"It is what it is," he said as he shrugged. "Frankly, I think I was always this way. But the concussion gave me an excuse to be an asshole and say whatever I want, whenever I want. It's been quite freeing."

He paused, looked around, and then began again, "Hey, Marshal, how far is this place?"

"Forty-five minutes," replied the driver, making eye contact with Elliot in the rearview mirror.

"Any chance we can stop at a gas station? I've got about twenty soldiers that have been asking me for Red Bulls and cigarettes since they found out what I was doing today."

"We can stop, but you can't go inside. Me or the photographer can buy what you need."

"Why's that?"

"Uniforms. Commander wants us to keep a low profile. Doesn't want locals seeing U.S. soldiers out and about."

"Unbelievable, this guy," Elliot protested. "What's he think could happen? I miss our old commander. Now *that* was a man I could follow. Or, if not follow, at least not bitch about. That was a man I wouldn't bitch about."

Elliot turned in his seat to face the photographer, holding up an empty duffel bag he had brought.

"Alright, photo-dude, I'm gonna need you to buy about sixty Red Bulls and a few cartons of cigarettes."

"Do they sell cigarettes by the carton in Slovenia? I haven't seen any."

"Then buy as many packs as you can with this," Elliot said as he dropped a wad of cash in the photographer's hand.

"Any preference on the cigarettes?"

"Whatever's cheapest. I'm just gonna sell 'em off. The joes back at camp will smoke about anything they can get their hands on."

"You got it."

"We'll stop on the way back," Marshall said from the front, looking over his shoulder into his blind spot as he entered the motorway from an on-ramp and sped up. "We're running late."

"I'll allow it, as long as we stop," Elliot replied.

He noticed Tadros staring out the window, taken by the run-down farmhouses tossed across the vast, rolling hillside.

"Like what you see, Tadros?" he asked.

"My wife would love it out here, sergeant. I should bring her out here sometime. Feels so different from Italy."

Elliot leaned over Tadros to survey the van's surroundings.

"All looks the same to me, Tadros," he said dismissively.

"You have a wife, Tadros?" Scheben asked with sincerity, a smile on his face.

"I do, sergeant. And a son we welcomed into the world just a few months ago."

"That's great. Congratulations. Tough missing these early months, though," Scheben offered.

"Does she have postpartum depression?" Elliot interrupted before Tadros could respond to Scheben.

Tadros blinked.

"What, sergeant?"

"Your wife. Is she depressed? My wife had terrible postpartum after her pregnancies, especially after the first. Better watch that broom, buddy."

"Broom, sergeant?"

"Give it a rest, man," Scheben said, nudging Elliot. "No need to worry him."

"Why should I watch out for a broom, sergeant?" Tadros asked again.

Scheben sighed.

"Well," Elliot said with mischief in his voice, "a broom that's leaning against the side of your house by the front door while you're gone signals to other soldiers who *aren't* gone that your wife is open to—how should I say this?—extramarital encounters."

Tadros tried to remain composed, but his furrowed eyebrows and wide eyes revealed that Elliot had gotten to him.

"Don't listen to him, Tadros," Scheben said. "He's just bitter his own marriage is in the gutter."

"It's true. Actually, the gutter would be an improvement for me and the wife. And it all started with my first kid and that damn broom. Came home early from an exercise back at Bragg one weekend. Found it right there, right under my porch light next to the door."

"You sure your marriage ills didn't actually start before that?" Scheben suggested. "You ever wax poetic about Romanian doms to your wife?"

"I'll have you know, sir, that I had a fairy-tale marriage until my wife played the broom card," Elliot countered with faux authenticity.

"There's no way the broom signal is a real thing," the photographer said from the back, a skeptical-yet-entertained look on his face.

"It's real, alright," came the slow, deep voice of Marshall.

"How would you know, Marshall? You married?" Elliot asked.

"I used to be. And that's all I'll say on the matter," he responded, his eyes not leaving the road in front of him.

"Well, shit. I think that proves my point," Elliot said victoriously.

"Next subject," Marshall said. "Better yet, what are you guys planning on talking to the students about today?"

"Haven't thought too deeply about it," Elliot replied. "Figured I'd wing it."

Tadros remained speechless. He seemed to be searching his thoughts for memories of a broom suspiciously placed around his front door.

"What age groups are we going to be talking to?" Scheben asked.

The photographer spoke up.

"I visited a neighboring school a few months ago with another battalion," he said. "You'll probably drop by a couple of classrooms throughout the day. Last time, they talked with younger kids. Seemed like fourth graders or fifth graders."

"Today will be different," Marshall instructed from the front. "There is a younger and an older wing of the schoolhouse we're visiting. The equivalent of an elementary school and a middle school. I believe you'll be speaking with the oldest class in the younger wing, but a few of the older wing students who have expressed interest in military service have also been invited to the classroom."

"Alright," Scheben replied as he nodded his head.

"The commander wants you to connect with the kids," Marshall added. "Talk about where you're from, your family, your hobbies. Talk about how much you love baseball and apple pie. Tell the kids what an honor it is to train alongside the Slovenian Armed Forces. And, just as importantly, bring up interoperability. But not *too* much."

He looked back at his passengers in the rearview mirror and noticed that Tadros was preoccupied, absent from the present conversation.

"Tadros!" he called out loudly.

"Yes, sergeant," Tadros replied, quickly looking up at the rearview mirror, a frantic look in his eyes.

"You know what interoperability is?"

"Uh, no…," he stammered. "I don't think I do, sergeant."

"Would someone like to inform young Tadros here what interoperability is?"

Tadros glanced toward his fellow passengers in the seats next to him.

"Interoperability is how your wife sees you and every other soldier in the U.S. Army," Elliot said with a wide smile across his face. "*Interoperable*. Any one of us can get the job done. Or maybe even two or three of us. At a time. More efficient that way."

"Would you shut the fuck up?" Scheben asked, admonishing Elliot before turning to Tadros and providing a better answer with a gentler tone. "Interoperability is what makes NATO the most powerful military alliance in the world. Dozens of militaries working together as a single machine."

"You understand, Tadros?" asked Marshall as he stared at the young soldier through the mirror.

"Yes, sergeant. I think so," he replied.

Tadros looked back to Scheben.

"But why talk about this with a bunch of kids?" he asked, slowly re-joining the conversation at hand, trying not to think about Elliot's degenerate answer.

"Because interoperability only works if every piece of the puzzle thinks it fits," Marshall added.

"Start 'em young, Tadros," Elliot said, winking. "No one is gonna to step up to the plate and take our bat if they don't feel invested in the game."

***

Crowding against a classroom window, several of the younger students watched as a black passenger van turned into their parking lot.

"*Američani so tukaj*," shouted a girl as she looked from the window back to her teacher.

"Yes, they are here. But remember," said a woman with gray, shoulder-length hair, "speak English for our guests so they can understand you today."

The students nodded.

"Yes, Mrs. Lesjak," came the scattered, collective voice of the group.

"Okay," she smiled. "Everyone, take your seats."

***

Walking from the small parking lot to the entrance of the school, the Americans met a Slovenian soldier with a thick, dark beard, who welcomed them with bottles of water.

"Very nice to see you, Sergeant Marshall," he said as the soldiers approached. "I hope you had a pleasant drive. Was the commander not able to come along today?"

"Unfortunately, he was not able to find the time," Marshall replied. "But he sends his greetings and wants to assure you that these are some of the finest soldiers in the battalion. They all have kids themselves and are eager to share about their lives with the students here."

"Fantastic," he responded, assessing the soldiers in front of him.

"But you? You have children?" he continued as his eyes paused on Tadros. "You look so young!"

"Yes, sir. I became a father quite recently."

"Americans," he replied with a chuckle. "Okay, come with me. Today, you're going to be talking to Mrs. Lesjak's fifth year class, with a few older students from the older wing."

Following him into the building, the soiled, pungent American soldiers, who hadn't showered in nearly a month, were greeted by teachers standing in the doorways of their classrooms. A trail of dried mud followed them down the hallway, falling from their boots onto the recently mopped floor. It was clear to them this was certainly the elementary wing of the school. Bright, multicolored maps and drawings hung on the walls above rows of lockers. A giant papier-mâché caterpillar danced above their heads, tied with twine to the soft hallway lights, and a poster board, fastened to the window of the door at the end of the hall, displayed a group of culturally diverse children holding hands around a globe, catching the attention of Scheben and the photographer because of its English text.

The well-groomed Slovenian stopped at the door of Mrs. Lesjak's classroom, knocked, and then entered with the Americans behind him.

"Good morning!" the Slovenian children shouted as they saw the soldiers walk through their door.

"Hey, kids!" Elliot responded, smiling from ear to ear. "How are you today?"

"Good," a handful of kids said.

Others only smiled or laughed; some showed little interest. A few of the older students from the older wing sat in the back of the classroom, far quieter than their much younger peers.

Scheben, Elliot, and Tadros took seats at the front, the children watching their every move. Marshall, the photographer, and the Slovenian quietly made their way along the perimeter of the room and found seats in the back. Opening his large backpack, the photographer took out a camera and a lens and fastened the two pieces together.

"First of all," Mrs. Lesjak began, "we would like to thank you for taking time out of your busy and important schedules to visit us. The children are quite excited to hear about your lives, where you come from in the States, and what you are doing here in Slovenia. Would the three of you like to begin by sharing your names and a bit about yourselves?"

"Sure, I can start," Elliot suggested as he raised his eyebrows high. "My name is Sergeant Elliot. I am an infantry soldier in the United States Army. I am from the great state of Texas, and I have three kids."

A boy sitting in the front row tepidly lifted his hand in the air, his pointer finger and pinky finger extending above the middle two. He wore a shy smile.

"Hey, hey!" Elliot cheered as he shot a Hook 'em Horns gesture back at the boy. "This guy knows!"

Elliot winked at the boy in the front as the other students quietly giggled.

After the other two soldiers introduced themselves, Mrs. Lesjak thanked them and said that the children had prepared questions they'd like to ask. She turned to the class and called on an eager student whose hand was raised.

"Yes, Ivan. Go ahead."

"Have you ever killed anyone?" blurted the impudent student and, judging by the reaction of the teacher, a known troublemaker.

"Ivan, r*ekel sem ti, da tega vprašanja ne postavljaš!*" Mrs. Lesjak promptly scolded.

She turned to face the Americans.

"I am very sorry," she continued. "I told him not to ask that question earlier. The question I *had* allowed him to ask was what you think of Slovenia and what an average day consists of while you are here."

"Sure, I can take that one," Scheben spoke up.

He turned toward the student who had asked the original question.

"And to answer your question, no. I haven't killed anyone. In fact, only one of us has ever deployed to a combat zone," he said, glancing at Elliot.

"You have not deployed?" the teacher questioned.

The soldiers shook their heads, all but Elliot.

"Well, you are all young. Perhaps one day. So, what do you think of Slovenia?"

"Personally, I love Slovenia," Scheben said as he moved forward in his seat. "It is a beautiful country, and I would like to see more of it."

"And what does a typical day look like for you here?"

"Our days are all very different when we're on rotation. We don't really have a typical day. Most of our time is spent teaching, or learning from, our Slovenian allies," he said, gesturing toward the children in front of him. "Maybe one day we'll teach about how we clear rooms. Another day we'll learn from the Slovenians how they operate their radios. And then we put all that learning into action when we conduct drills or exercises in a simulated, wartime environment."

"Very good," the teacher said.

She turned toward one of the older students sitting in the back of the classroom with his hand raised. His polo shirt was buttoned to the top, and his backpack contained twice as many books as any of his peers' did.

"Yes, Andrej. Go ahead."

"What is the purpose of conducting exercises together in a simulated environment of war?" he asked as he lowered his hand and cocked his head to the side.

"Yeah, I can get this one," Elliot said.

"Basically," he continued, "NATO is this strong alliance of militaries. We help each other and make each other stronger. If we share our knowledge with you guys, and you guys share your knowledge with us, we're both better for it."

"Of course I know what NATO is," the Slovenian student responded to Elliot. "I am trying to ask a different question. I will phrase it another way."

He paused for a moment, collecting his thoughts as Scheben and Elliot exchanged looks.

"What I want to know is," he continued, "is it not enough for our very high-ranking military leaders to be able to work together? For example, to determine which missions the Slovenians undertake and which missions the Americans undertake? How likely is it that our two militaries would need to work together on a small scale, where individual soldiers must work together?"

"That's a very good question," Scheben said, taking over for Elliot. "The truth is, even though our two militaries may never be integrated on a small scale in real combat, we need to be prepared for the possibility, regardless. Pooling our resources and sharing our infrastructure now gives us the option to do the same thing later, if we need to."

"And if our interests diverge?" the student asked.

"What do you mean?"

"Our militaries can be co-dependent if the partners involved behave as a single organism with the same interests. What happens when this is not the case? What happens if some interests attract the attention of an allied partner, but not the attention of the… but not the attention of the…," he paused, biting his lip in frustration. "I cannot recall the word."

He looked at the floor.

"Universal!" he exclaimed after remembering the word he'd searched for. "What happens if particular interests attract the attention of an allied partner, but not the attention of the universal whole?"

The Americans exchanged additional looks among themselves.

"Young man," Scheben replied after clearing his throat, "you are asking questions that are way, way above my pay grade. Thankfully, I don't have to think about that kind of stuff. I'm a soldier, not a politician."

The student bowed his head in Scheben's direction, thanking him for his answer.

"Your English is unbelievable. Hell, I'd say it's even better than mine," Elliot remarked as the students in the classroom laughed.

He turned toward Mrs. Lesjak.

"Do they learn English in school?"

"Yes, of course," she replied. "They begin learning English from the first year. It is very important for them. In this district, they have the option to go to a business-oriented tertiary school, and if they choose this, their English must be perfect to succeed in that field."

She looked out across the classroom full of students and smiled, and then she turned back to the soldiers.

"Have you, by chance, learned any Slovenian since being here?" she asked.

"Unfortunately, I can't say I have," Scheben said.

"I learned one word," began Elliot. "What was it...? One of the Slovenian soldiers taught it to me."

He looked at the floor and scratched his head.

"Shra... something? Shranjo...?" he stumbled.

The teacher's eyes grew wide.

"*Sranje!*" he yelled.

Mrs. Lesjak gasped, and the classroom burst into laughter.

"It's *sranje!* That's it. What's that word mean?"

"I don't think that word has ever been uttered within these halls," she said slowly, after throwing a harsh look at the students still laughing. "Best not repeat that word, Mr. Elliot."

After bringing the classroom back into order, Mrs. Lesjak called on each and every one of the students, in turn, who had prepared questions for their American guests. As the pace of the interrogation gradually slowed to a stop, Mrs. Lesjak turned to face Tadros.

"Mr. Tadros, you cannot be a single day over nineteen years old."

"You're right, ma'am," he replied. "This is my first duty station. Came here straight from airborne school. I turn nineteen in a month."

"Then you were only a small child when the towers fell. Your country has been at war in the Middle East for most of your life. I am curious, if you don't mind the question, why did you choose to join the military?"

Tadros took a deep breath, and then he looked at the many students waiting for his reply.

"When I was about your age," he began, "Egypt went through a revolution. I wasn't old enough to understand what revolution meant or why revolution was happening, but what I do remember, and what stuck with me after seeing the scenes from Tahrir Square on the news, was that Egyptians were desperate. They were desperate for something new, anything but what they had. They were willing to risk their lives and everything they owned for the smallest chance of change...."

He paused and turned his face to Mrs. Lesjak.

"Why had I gotten so lucky?" he asked.

She raised an eyebrow.

"You see," he said, turning back to the students, "my parents left Egypt and moved to the United States just before I was born. I'm an American citizen because they saw what was happening in their country and they made a decision to leave."

The children became quite silent as every eye in the classroom rested on Tadros.

"In our Declaration of Independence, it was written that governments are created to secure the rights of people who live *within* their borders. But what about those who don't? What role does a country like the U.S. have in fighting for the rights of people who don't live within our borders, especially when their own governments oppress them?"

Mrs. Lesjak watched him with a calm smile.

"I didn't join the U.S. Army to make the world safer for democracy. I don't even know what that means. I joined because I didn't know what else I could do. And I had to do something."

He looked down and continued in a lower voice.

"And I do believe I am doing what is right."

The room remained silent for a few moments.

"I hope you find what you are looking for," Mrs. Lesjak said softly to him.

She turned slowly toward the students.

"I think our American friends must be going. They have a long drive ahead of them. Are there any last questions?"

A single hand shot up from a girl in a blue dress, sitting by herself at the side of the room.

"Yes, Valerija. Your question?"

"You said earlier you have a daughter a little older than us," she said, directing her inquiry at Scheben.

"Yes, that's right."

"Do you miss her?"

"I would do anything to see her right now," he responded.

Tears flooded her eyes, and within seconds she began to sob. Rising from her desk, she rushed out of the classroom, letting the door slam behind her.

"I must apologize for Valerija," Mrs. Lesjak said to a bewildered Scheben. "Her father is in Iraq with a NATO force, ensuring a smooth process in this year's parliamentary elections."

"Her dad is in Iraq?" Scheben asked.

"Yes, his second deployment in the past four years."

On the way back to the base, the soldiers stopped for Red Bulls and cigarettes.

Nobody Passes Here

The mountains were blue, and the air was cold and still at that dark, early morning hour. A single, winding road connected two towns that lay on opposite sides of the greatly elevated, narrow pass in the icy Dolomites of Northern Italy, cascading into the south of the Alps. A shepherd moved a flock of sheep from one pasture to another, each sheep equipped with a bell around its neck lest it sneak away in the direction of a cliff, and a young man in a '99 Fiat Barchetta roadster pulled to the side of the road, parking next to a closed, wooden lodge and the passing sheep. He saw a group of mountaineers. Some of these mountaineers looked to him to be around his father's age, some much older. They stood gathered around a few cars, headlights on, a single raven feather sticking from each of their green, felt hats.

He left his car and stepped onto the grass, mere paces away from the foot of a mountain peak that towered over every nearby thing, an Alpine fortress standing guard over ancient ridges. The man raised his eyes to the peak. His crooked nose sat prominent between freckled cheeks, now red from the cold, and he wore a distressed jacket over a thick, wool sweater, a black ball cap over his ginger hair. He turned back to look at the feather-hatted individuals by the cars, all of them staring back at him, whispering among themselves, greatly interested in the curious visitor.

"*Buongiorno!*" one of the men in the mountaineering group called out to him.

"*Buongiorno,*" the young man replied with the heaviest American accent.

"*Sei qui per guardare l'alba?*" the mountaineer asked.

"I'm sorry," he said, walking in their direction. "My Italian is not very good. Do any of you speak English?"

"*Inglese? Sì*," the one who'd been speaking replied, patting the back of the man next to him.

The appointed individual stepped to the front of the group. His face was narrow. He had kind, inquisitive eyes, and with both hands he held a thick salami in front of him, the end already cut into. He chewed what was in his mouth and then spoke.

"You are here to watch the sunrise?" he asked, swallowing. "And you are an American?"

"That's right," he replied. "Yes to both."

"Good! Then you have come to the right place!" he exclaimed as he lifted the salami above his head. "You will not find a better sunrise in all of Italy. May I ask, how did you come to know of this place in the mountains? It is not a *popular* destination."

"One of my friends let me in on the secret. Said I had to see it before I leave. That it would change my life. I've saved it for my last weekend in Italy."

"How long have you been here?"

"Almost three years. I'm stationed in Vicenza with the U.S. Army, but on Thursday, I'm finished. I'll be a civilian again."

"Will you go back to the United States?" the Italian asked.

"I don't think so," the ginger replied. "The Army gave me a one-way ticket back to Maine, where I grew up, but I'm not boarding that plane."

"You will stay in Italy?"

"My plan is to drive east toward the Balkans until I find someone to buy my car. Then, I'll take my backpack and walk to the closest train station. From there, I'll make my way to Istanbul, and by New Year's Eve, I'd like to be in India, maybe even Nepal."

The young ginger spoke with a calm resignation. Though the American was clearly eager to begin his travels, the Italian sensed a sadness in the soon-to-be-discharged soldier, an acceptance that much was about to be left behind and that, after Thursday, everything would be different for him.

"You are between two chapters in your life," the Italian said to the boy, cooly, before a pause, a deep breath, and a smile. "There is a ridge behind this hill."

The Italian turned and pointed up toward the dark sky.

"There is no trail," he continued. "Did your friend tell you how to get to the top?"

"He didn't."

"In this case, you must join us. We will guide you through the pass and make sure your last weekend in this country is made special by our sunrise," he said, transferring the salami to his left hand and raising the other for a handshake. "What do you say? Will you join us?"

The American smiled and shook the man's hand.

"Thank you for the invitation," he said. "I would love to join you."

"*Bene!*"

The Italian turned to his friends, who were watching but did not understand a word of what had been said, and quickly rattled off a couple sentences.

A stumpy fellow with a droopy face emerged from the back of the group with a knife in hand. He casually motioned to the one who'd been talking with their new guest.

"*Vieni qua.*"

The man with the salami set the meat on the hood of one of the cars, turning back toward the American ginger and winking at him. Lifting the knife to the meat, the stumpy fellow cut several slices from the end of the salami. He proceeded to grab one of the slices with his finger and thumb and then raised it above his head, walking toward their guest.

"*Qua,*" he said. "*Mangia.*"

The young ginger raised his eyebrows and looked at the Italian who spoke English.

"He wants you to eat the *sopressa*," the Italian said.

"And what exactly is… *sopressa?*" asked the ginger.

"This is *sopressa vicentina!* The *sopressa* is an aged meat. Pork, to be exact, with spices and fat. Made here in the north and known in all of Italy. But the *sopressa vicentina* is the very best of all the *sopressi*. And this *sopressa vicentina* was made by Luca himself! From a pig he raised from birth!"

The stumpy Luca brought the slice above their guest's head and delicately placed it on his tongue, eagerly awaiting a reaction.

"My god," the ginger said after chewing. "This is delicious."

"*Deliziosa?*" asked Luca, turning toward the group's translator.

"*Sì, deliziosa,*" he confirmed to Luca.

"*Deliziosa!*" Luca joyously exclaimed as he turned back to their guest, throwing his arm around the unprepared American and gently bringing him close to Luca's face.

Luca pinched the fingers of his right hand together into a finger purse gesture and continued in a frustrated tone.

"*Come può aver senso? Ascoltami. Questa è la ricetta di mio nonno. Ha la migliore sopressa vicentina di tutta la provincia, ma siccome faceva non abito a Vicenza non posso vendere la mia sopressa come sopressa vicentina. Devo cambiare il nome. Ma non lo farò! Questa è la sopressa vicentina, la migliore del nord!*"

"What is he saying?" asked the ginger, looking to the narrow-faced translator.

"He is mad that he cannot sell his *sopressa vicentina*. It is the recipe of his grandfather, who was known throughout the province of Vicenza for making the very best *sopressa vicentina*. But because Luca now lives in the province of Trento, he cannot sell his *sopressa vicentina* unless he changes the name. But he refuses."

"Why does he need to change the name if he wants to sell it?"

"It is a protected food under the European Union. Brussels will not allow anyone to sell *sopressa vicentina* unless it is made in the province of Vicenza."

"Why does the European Union care who sells the *sopressa?*"

"It is to protect the authentic *sopressa vicentina*, which, according to Brussels, cannot possibly be made outside of Vicenza."

"*Ma vaffanculo,*" the stumpy *sopressa* maker grumbled, shaking his fist and grimacing.

"Enough about the *sopressa*," concluded the translator. "We must go to the top of the hill. It is the only place to watch the sun come into the pass."

"Wait," said the ginger, "who are you guys, anyway?"

"Forgive me for abandoning the introductions! This is part of our annual reunion. Years ago, we were the protectors of these mountains. We were, and forever will be, the *Alpini*. Mountain soldiers!"

Upon hearing the word "*Alpini*," one of the men in the group shouted, "*Di qui non si passa!*" as he shut the trunk of his car and activated the light in his headlamp. "*Andiamo!*"

"The *Alpini*," replied the ginger to his host. "I've heard of you guys before. Are you airborne?"

"No. Are you airborne?"

"Yeah, I'm airborne."

"Airborne, it is nice to meet you! I am Marco," said the translator. "You have already met Luca. In the back, by the cars, that is Giuseppe. And that is Roberto, and there is Stefano and Ale. Rinaldo is the old one."

Each individual responded with either a "*ciao*" or a "*piacere*" as Marco called out their names, except for Rinaldo, who grunted.

The ginger laughed.

"Okay," he said. "Nice to meet all of you, too."

"*Andiamo!*"

After shutting the trunks of the other cars and grabbing their packs, the group moved in the opposite direction of the Alpine fortress, toward a high, grassy hilltop, one nestled within ridges full of smaller, shorter peaks on every side. It was still dark, and the trail up the hill was rocky. Had they not been wearing headlamps, they would certainly have tripped on the rocks at multiple points. Though the sun still crouched low beneath the choppy, mountainous ridge behind the hill, its slow approach sent luminescent specks toward the ether that bounced back to the earth and brought a small amount of indirect light to the pass. Blues and grays transformed into pinks and greens. One by one, each man turned off his headlamp.

"*A metà strada!*" one of them called out.

Marco turned toward their guest.

"He said we are halfway there!"

The ginger nodded, though Marco noticed the American was breathing heavier than the rest.

"Are you okay, airborne?"

"Yeah," he replied with difficulty. "I'm okay. Halfway there."

"Halfway there," repeated Marco.

An *Alpino* near the front started to sing, and, after a couple seconds, the rest of the group joined in like a choir.

"*Dai fidi tetti del villaggio i bravi alpini son partiti, mostran la forza ed il coraggio della lor salda gioventù,*" they sang as they hiked up the hill.

Marco dropped back to walk alongside their struggling guest.

"What are they singing?" the ginger asked through labored breaths.

"This is the song of the *Alpini*. It is very old. From before the Great War. Written by Camillo Fabiano."

"What does it mean?"

Marco held his finger in the air and perked up his ears, listening for which verse his comrades were singing.

"Yes. Just now, they sang something like, 'The good-looking soldiers are from the Alps with very strong youth and their bold chest breathes in a great sense of pride!'"

The *Alpini* belted their battle hymn, matching the step of their march to the rhythm of the song.

"*Là tra le selve ed i burroni, là tra le nebbie fredde e il gelo, piantan con forza i lor picconi le vie rendon più brevi. E quando il sole brucia e scalda le cime e le profondità, il fiero Alpino scruta e guarda, pronto a dare il 'Chi va là?'*"

"And with this," Marco continued, "they said something like, 'There in the woods and the,' how do you say... 'canyon?' Is 'canyon' a word?"

"Yeah. A canyon is like a big, rocky valley or a gorge or something."

"Okay, perfect. So, they sang, 'There in the woods and the canyon, there in the coldness and the ice, they forcefully swing their tools, and they make the way shorter.' It means," he said as he scrunched his eyebrows and searched for the proper way to explain, "that we *Alpini* are breaking through the ice and snow to make the path shorter for other troops to get to the frontline. Like some of your combat engineers. But we are also the other troops! We are both combat engineer as well as the frontline fighter. Then, in the last verse, they sang, 'And when the sun comes and warms the highs and lows of the mountains, the proud *Alpino* soldier turns and says to any intruder: *Who goes there?*'"

The ginger looked back at him with a blank expression. His face had lost what little color it normally had, and he breathed heavily though his wide, open mouth.

"*Ohi*," Marco said. "Are you okay?"

"I think I need to lie down," he replied shakily, his legs wavering.

"*Oddio,*" Marco mumbled as he stabilized the ginger and brought him gently to the ground. "Just take a rest. Here, drink some water."

As Marco opened a bottle of water and handed it down to the ginger, old Rinaldo shouted from the front of the group.

"*Dobbiamo continuare a muoverci o mancheremo l'alba.*"

"*Ci siamo quasi. Non la mancheremo,*" Marco shouted back.

Rinaldo sighed, staring at their burdensome guest with a scowl on his face.

"What did he say?" the ginger asked.

"He wants us to keep moving. But, it is okay. You can rest for a minute."

"I'm sorry, Marco," said the ginger. "This came out of nowhere."

"It is okay," replied Marco, a long smile on his narrow face. "You are an airborne paratrooper, so you are familiar with high altitude. But you are an airborne paratrooper, so you are not familiar with eating *sopressa* and then hiking in the high altitude!"

The ginger laughed.

"I guess you're right about that," he said. "Please, go on without me. I can watch the sunrise from here. It's already an amazing view. We can meet up again when you come back down."

"Absolutely not. I am your guide. We will finish this together."

"I really don't know if I can. Too lightheaded. About to puke."

"Give me your bag," Marco said as he reached out his hand.

The ginger moved his head quickly upwards toward his host.

"You already have a bag. I can't let you take mine, too!"

"I have been carrying heavy things in these mountains my entire life. Please, give me your bag. I think you can finish this hill if you must only carry the weight of your body. Now, come on! We finish this!"

The ginger remained reluctant, but, after a moment, he nodded and handed over his pack.

"*Grazie*," the American ginger said.

Marco chuckled.

The pass was now brighter, and everyone could see their surroundings as clear as the day, but the sun had not yet peered over the ridge behind the hill. Though it was brighter, it was also colder than before. The men zipped up their jackets to their chins, and those with scarves tightened them around their necks.

As the group arrived at the top of the large, grassy hill, a stunning vista came into view. The ridge that hid the approaching sun lay to their left. To their right, a sea of peaks stretched out across the spiking and cascading landscape, the tallest peaks capped with snow and already adorned with crowns of sunlight. The lower peaks were hazy and purple, and the lowest of them all were still immersed in the shadowy, morning mist so typical of mountain valleys.

"You're right," said the ginger as the group began dropping their packs onto the ground and taking in the scene around them. "This is a beautiful sunrise. Thank you for bringing me up here."

"Airborne, this is not the sunrise!" Marco said. "We have a few minutes! I am glad you are looking better. Life and color has returned to your face."

"I feel much better. And thank you for taking my bag."

"It was my duty as your guide in these mountains! Honor demanded it."

Old Rinaldo wandered toward the two as they talked. The hair that poked out from beneath his feathered, felt hat was white, as was his mustache, which he kept meticulously trimmed and tidy. For the first time, the American ginger noticed how old Rinaldo really was, and was impressed by the fact he hiked up the hill so easily. He felt ashamed he'd held the group up, being young, as well as the only one who was still a soldier.

"*Rinaldo, come stai?*" asked Marco.

"*Chiedigli se ha disegnato peni su qualche monumento ultimamente,*" old Rinaldo said.

Marco smirked, shyly, hiding his face from the ginger and putting his hand on the back of the elderly man.

"*Sii gentile con il nostro ospite, Rinaldo,*" Marco said quietly.

"What did he say?"

Both of the Italians looked at the ginger. Marco stalled, rambling under his breath and moving his hands in a great commotion as he considered how best to navigate what Rinaldo had said for their guest.

"Rinaldo asked," began Marco, blinking like a fish out of water, "if you have drawn any *penises* on monuments lately."

"Penises?" the ginger blurted, caught off guard. "No, I haven't been drawing penises on monuments lately. Or anything on monuments lately! Or anything on monuments anytime in the past!"

Old Rinaldo swung his gaze to Marco.

"*Dice che non è stato lui,*" said Marco. "*Ovviamente. È un bravo ragazzo!*"

"If he wants to know who is drawing that stuff on monuments, it's probably only one or two soldiers. They make us all look bad. Trust me, we hate whoever is doing that just as much as you do!"

"He knows that, airborne," replied Marco. "You have to forgive Rinaldo. His father was killed by the Americans in Garfagnana. Of course, this was very many years ago, but Rinaldo does not even remember his father; he has no memories of him at all. It is difficult, I am sure, for him."

"Garfagnana? What is that?" the ginger asked.

"From the *seconda guerra mondiale*.... The—how do you say it—Second World War? You Americans invaded from the south. His father was killed during the advance as you traveled north up our peninsula."

"My god," said the ginger. "I don't know what to say. I'm sorry his father died."

Old Rinaldo stood by, watching the two closely as they spoke.

"*Garfagnana? Parli della Garfagnana?*" he asked.

"*Sì, Rinaldo. Va bene. Cerca di rilassarti,*" said Marco.

Old Rinaldo brought his hand to the brim of his hat, removing it and bringing it down to his side. With his other hand, he stroked his eyebrows and then looked at Marco, a tired, slightly exasperated look on his face.

"*Gli Alpini non sarebbero mai dovuti essere in Garfagnana, siamo stati usati da un fascista che non si curava di noi. Come se fossimo usati ora in Afghanistan. Siamo i protettori delle Alpi, questo è il nostro posto.*"

The ginger looked to Marco, who was facing old Rinaldo, an endearing expression on Marco's face as he listened to his elder, Rinaldo.

"What did Rinaldo say?" the ginger asked.

"He said the *Alpini* should never have been in Garfagnana," replied Marco, turning back to their guest. "We are the protectors of the Alps, mountain soldiers. Our expertise was used in those years, used to fight for a cause that many of us did not believe in."

"Did he mention something about Afghanistan?"

"He did," Marco said, slowly nodding his head. "Rinaldo does not believe we have any interests to be found in Afghanistan. He does not know why we are there. You see, like Garfagnana, Afghanistan has many mountains. He believes we are being exploited and that we must protect our homeland here in our *own* mountains, not travel to the other side of the world to fight a war we do not fully understand."

The ginger looked down, feeling a pinch of embarrassment. Or shame? He couldn't tell. But he knew he was uncomfortable.

"Are all of you from the mountains?" he asked, looking back up to the men and quickly averting his eyes from Rinaldo in favor of a more accepting Marco.

"This is what makes the *Alpini* special. The great majority of our soldiers are recruited from the Dolomites, and if not from the mountains themselves, at least from the regions of the north."

"Then the strong soldiers with boldness in their chests are really from these Alps," the ginger said with a small smile on his face. "Like your song says."

"Yes! The song is true!"

The other *Alpini* veterans called out to their comrades that the sun was very near.

"Come, airborne," said Marco. "You will not want to miss this."

Marco, Rinaldo, and the ginger walked toward the rest of the group and stood facing the ridge behind the hill. The morning light was on full display, but the sun still hid. The earth rotated on its axis the smallest fraction of a degree more, and, instantly, through the lowest point on the choppy ridge, a single shaft of brilliant light broke from one side to the other and pierced the mist that swirled atop the hill inside the pass. The light descended upon the face of the Alpine fortress that dwarfed them all. The shadows that danced upon its uneven face were all exposed and made to flee the lurid sunlight, and the group found themselves inside a pass now made of pure gold. The air, the rocks, the grass, and even the sheep below. All of it.

The ginger gawked, letting out several quick breaths, as if in disbelief. He looked at Marco, whose smile from ear to ear told the story of how deeply he adored these mountains.

"I told you," Marco said to the ginger with a wink. "Yes?"

A loud thump shot through the air from one of the *Alpini* soldiers to the ginger's left. He turned his head toward the sound and saw a long stream of white wine arching through the gleaming sky, catching and refracting little pieces of sunlight that poured into the pass. The *Alpini* cheered.

"Prosecco," Marco said. "The best sparkling wine in the entire world. Only made here in the north of Italy. Much better than champagne. Much, much better."

The *Alpini* shared the wine between eight glasses, raising a toast to the sunrise. When they killed the wine, one of them pulled a bottle of grappa from his pack and passed it down the line, each taking swigs straight from the bottle. As the sun continued to rise, they stood in silence on the hill, passing the bottle of grappa back and forth.

"It is beautiful, airborne, yes?" Marco whispered to the ginger.

"It is."

"We belong to these mountains, and these mountains belong to us. We are willing to die protecting them and the places we have built here. And indeed, many of us have. But there is nothing more noble than giving your life for the people, and the land, that you love."

Slowly, each member of the group picked up his pack and prepared for the journey back down the hill. As they descended, they sang their sad melodies for battles and lovers either won or lost in years gone by.

The ginger paused at the top of the hill.

After a few meters, Marco turned around and called up to him. From Marco's perspective, the ginger was dark and silhouetted against the light.

"*Andiamo*, airborne! There is still much prosecco to be drunk before you depart on your new adventures!"

The ginger smiled. He turned, briefly, to face the ridge and the risen sun.

"Goodbye, Italy," he said before starting down the hill. "I will miss you."

Go the Spoils

Go the Spoils

The night was silent, as silent as nights come, except for the occasional bat that screeched and swooped in search of prey and the cool, autumn wind that whistled through the trees in the midnight forest. Two headlights provided two soldiers the comfort of concealment, as when one watches an evening scene lit by street-lamps unfold from the safety of a dark apartment. There is a certain peace available to those on the giving end of a bright light, a feeling of protection imbued by the idea that you can see them, but they cannot see you, especially in a vast, dark place.

That's how Specialist McAdam felt riding in the passenger seat alongside Specialist Johnson as the two crept along the tight, meandering roads of Hohenfels Training Area, Germany, and, more specifically, that huge swath of uninhabited land designated only for war games known as the *Box*, a daunting, wooded area with a long memory and a troubled past.

Mick, as he was known, turned his head from the window to Specialist Johnson.

Johnson was a petite solider, with tan skin and dark hair that she kept in a bun on the back of her head. Despite her stature, she drove, and lived, with the confidence of someone who knew the world and everything in it was hers for the taking. She was relaxed, as if she knew those things would simply come to her with time.

Mick saw that quality in her, and he respected it. He was quite fond of himself in many ways, but, in his heart, he was insecure about his place in the world, and if he were to be psychoanalyzed by a professional, he might have been told he was deep in the throes of imposter syndrome.

There was an urgency in the way Mick lived his life, but he preferred not to show it. He liked to exude calmness, constructing an image of a man who approached daunting circumstances in stride, but truly, this photographer, whose photos had been published more times than many of his peers combined, felt hesitant about his work and the way his résumé stacked up against those of fellow photographers.

"I know this is the 173rd we're dealin' with this week, but we really should've asked a platoon leader where this attack is supposed to be happenin' tonight," Mick said to Johnson. "Opposing force is still occupying half the Box. Could happen anywhere."

She glanced at him, a smile on her face.

"And spoil all the fun?" Johnson asked. "And if I know the 173rd, they'll assume we're in bed with OPFOR and give us bad coordinates."

"Well, they'd be right about that, wouldn't they?" Mick poked. "At least for one of us."

Johnson's smile opened, and she gaped at Mick, a look of mock-anger and surprise on her face.

"I won't tell you these things if you're gonna come at me like that!" she shot back.

She rattled the vehicle into second gear and quickly accelerated toward the next turn in the road. Just before reaching the bend, she popped the clutch and pulled the emergency brake, whipping the vehicle 180 degrees.

When the vehicle came to a stop, within a cloud of kicked-up dust, Johnson immediately sped up and then looked to her right to find Mick biting his lip, holding back a tight smile.

"You know I love comin' out to the Box with you, Johnson, but tonight is our best night to catch a gunfight with these guys. Let's not screw around. It'll be hard enough to find 'em; these guys take this shit seriously."

"As every brigade combat team should," Johnson suggested. "This can make or break a commander's career."

A sputtering noise from the engine interrupted Johnson. The car slowed.

"We out of gas?" Mick asked.

"No. We've got half a tank."

Another unsettling noise arose from the engine as the peddle response and the power steering gave out. The vehicle rolled to a stop.

Johnson slammed the palm of her hand against the steering wheel.

"Piece of shit…," she muttered.

The headlights flickered off, leaving them in total darkness.

"Why'd ya' kill the lights?" Mick asked, a chill traveling down his spine.

"I didn't. The car's dead," she responded, trying to turn the engine back over. "Useless."

She looked at Mick.

"Let's hope it wasn't the Box Witch," she said with a half-smile.

"The what?" Mick asked.

"You serious?" Johnson asked, surprised. "You haven't heard of the witch of Hohenfels?"

"I've been stationed here longer than you have, Johnson, and I never once heard of a witch of Hohenfels."

"That's because you hang out with nerds," she replied.

"You're in quite the mood tonight."

"I'm sorry, Mick."

She paused.

"Let's just grab the radios and call the shop," she went on.

Mick could feel his ears become red and warm as Johnson turned in her seat to grab a pack that was, usually, in the seat behind her own.

She swung back toward Mick.

"Where's the pack?" she asked.

Mick delayed, and then he scratched the back of his head.

"Mick?"

"There's a small chance I might have forgotten to load the pack before we left," he said, his eyebrows raised.

"This is just great," Johnson snapped at him.

"I told you," Mick said through an embarrassed half-grin, trying to avoid her wrath (which could sometimes be severe), "I had a late one last night. Haven't been firin' on all cylinders today."

"And what good are these cylinders gonna do for us while we're stuck on the far side of the Box, no cell service, in a shit van?" she spat at him.

"Listen, Johnson. We'll wait the night out. By mornin', they'll notice the van's not in the lot and send someone after us. As long as we stay together, I promise I won't let this Box Bitch eat ya'."

Johnson puffed lightly though her nose in subdued amusement.

"The Box Witch, Mick," she said with a little smile.

Johnson then shook her head in his direction and exhaled more forcefully, disarmed by Mick's ability to say *just* the right thing at the right time.

"What would you do without me?" she continued.

She looked out of the window, accepting the fact that they'd be stuck in the Box for the night.

"Wood line or van?" she asked.

"I'd say we bunk down in the wood line," Mick responded. "I wouldn't want to wake up to our dark van getting bulldozed by a blackout convoy of Humvees on their way to the attack tonight."

"Fair enough."

She opened the driver's side door. As she did so, the lights in the van turned on. Mick felt exposed, and he quickly joined Johnson at the rear of the vehicle.

He thought it was strange that the inside lights turned on while the rest of the vehicle was in such a state of disrepair.

They opened the doors, and each grabbed a flashlight from a bag. As Johnson pointed it at the wood line and started in its direction, Mick leaned in and picked up two of the softer bags in the van he thought they could use as impromptu pillows.

The woods were dense, and Johnson had not gone far when Mick caught up to her. She was standing still. Mick didn't know why. Her flashlight remained trained on a single point.

"Look," she whispered.

A ruined edifice of stone and wood, convoluted by the many trees growing in and around its walls, slowly came into Mick's view as his eyes adjusted to the forest and the flashlight.

"Just another old castle or random church in Hohenfels," Johnson suggested as the two moved their flashlights across the crumbling structure.

"This, Johnson, was a church. The bell tower gives it away," Mick responded as he gestured his light up and down a mostly intact tower toward the back of the dilapidated ruins.

Approaching the building from its side, Mick and Johnson paused and gazed at the crumbling walls and the battered tower. It looked as if, long ago, the place had once been quite beautiful. Now, it was in ruins with a caved-in roof. Vines and ivy grew across its surface, and there was evidence that a variety of animals had made this rubble their home. They walked around to the front, where the wall was partially destroyed, leaving the structure open for them to enter. After throwing the light into each corner of the room, Johnson carefully stepped over several fallen stones and entered the chapel, followed by a slightly more tentative Mick.

"If this place could tell us its stories," Mick said after finding his bearings and identifying the best exit routes.

"Maybe this is where the witch lived," Johnson suggested.

Mick sighed.

"Alright, Johnson. What's the witch all about?"

She smiled.

"You know this place was a Nazi base, right?" she started. "We took it from the Germans toward the end of the war."

"Yeah, of course," Mick replied. "Like most of our bases here in Germany, the enlisted men went running for the hills as the officers barricaded themselves in their offices and blew their own heads off."

He sat down on a large stone and looked up through the missing roof at the tower set against stars and a matte black sky.

"And with that," Mick continued, "these woods passed from one kingdom to the next."

Johnson joined Mick on a nearby stone opposite his.

"During the war, the Germans used this place to keep all kinds of prisoners," Johnson said. "Gypsies and Jews. They were brought here, and I can only imagine what they went through."

Mick gazed at her skeptically.

"Go on," he said.

"They say the Box Witch is the spirit of one of the Gypsies who was tortured and killed in Hohenfels. And now she haunts the Box, trying to take her revenge on anyone wearing a uniform."

"Who's 'they?'" Mick asked. "Who says this stuff?"

Johnson smiled.

"It's base lore," she replied. "Lots of people."

Mick laughed.

"I know what you're thinking," Johnson said, playfully. "You're thinking I'm just trying to freak you out, here in the middle of the woods."

"And it's not gonna work!" Mick replied as he continued laughing at what he thoroughly believed to be Johnson's poor attempt at a joke.

"I'm only telling you what I've been told!" she went on.

The mood was light, both Mick and Johnson acting flirtatiously with one another in the dark.

"Okay, I'll take the bait," Mick said. "Who's seen her, and what do they say about her?"

"OPFOR sees her all the time. It's a thing. There are parts of the Box the guys won't even go to anymore. On purpose, at least."

"They go there against their will?"

"They just end up there. One minute they're driving around the mock towns in the south, and the next minute they've found themselves all the way up by Hohenburg and have the feeling they're being watched from the wood line. Then they speed their ass back down to garrison and get out of the Box ASAP. This happens regularly."

"This is a dense forest, and it gets dark at night. Normal to lose track of where you are."

"Lose track of where you are? That's a forty-minute drive. And being watched?"

"It sounds like your boyfriend is messing with you."

Johnson paused, and she sighed softly.

"We're not dating, Mick."

"I'm sorry," he said, looking down. "Your friend."

The conversation having come to a grinding halt, Mick studied the layer of dirt and grass that stretched across the patchwork of old stones that once formed the floor. He remembered that in parts of medieval Europe it was common for the members of a church to be buried beneath its stones, close to the alter if you were lucky, and he wondered if that had been done here.

"It's not just OPFOR," Johnson said, breaking the silence.

"What?"

"The safeties have a story about the witch, too."

Mick looked up at her with a soft expression that signaled he meant for her to continue and that he'd be more willing to hear her out, gentler on her complicated social life.

"A platoon of MPs was on a patrol at dusk," she began. "Based on the intelligence they'd collected, there wasn't supposed to be any OPFOR in the area. As soon as the light was gone, a few trucks in the back of the convoy heard someone knocking on their doors. That's not really something the OPFOR guys here would do, but the MPs responded like it was the opposing force. They checked the area and found no one, and then they told one of the Box safeties about it. When he confirmed with the other safeties that there wasn't any opposing force in the area, they paused the exercise and had the entire area searched, assuming a local German had snuck onto the post. They didn't find anyone."

"And the safeties think it was the witch?"

"The next day, one of the safeties claimed he'd been visited in his dreams by a young woman. She wore tattered clothes and seemed to be asking him questions, but he couldn't understand anything she was saying. He told one of his buddies who'd been working with him the night before. Turns out both safeties had the same dream. Pretty damn creepy."

"It's a decent ghost story, Johnson. But there's a problem."

Johnson raised an eyebrow.

"The Nazis used this place as a POW camp for Brits, mostly," Mick stated confidently but respectfully. "Gypsies and Jews *did* live here, but not 'til we took it from the Germans. When the war was over, we used Hohenfels as a refugee camp while we tried to figure out what to do with all the prisoners we'd just inherited."

Johnson remained silent for a few moments while she reflected on the implications of Mick's info.

"You sure about that?" she finally asked.

"Yep," Mick replied with a nod.

"That would mean that if a Gypsy was tortured and died here, it happened under the Americans?"

"Bit of a wrench in the narrative," Mick said with a smile. "Just another reason not to believe in ghost stories."

"There's no way that could have happened."

"Then change the legend," Mick suggested.

"Yeah, we won the war," she said, tongue in cheek. "Don't we get to write the stories?"

"Now we're talkin'," Mick responded as he rubbed his hands together.

The flirting had resumed.

"What else do you know about this place?" Johnson asked. "If there's a witch here, what dark era can we say she's from?"

Mick looked back to the stones on the ground, furrowing his eyebrows as he thought about the history of Hohenfels.

"The Velburg stuff is pretty weird," he said.

"The Velburg stuff?"

"And the murderous peasant girl. That'd actually work damn well for our purposes."

"I'm intrigued."

"You ever been all the way to the eastern edge of the Box? By the cliffs and the secret exit toward Velburg?" he asked.

"There's not much over there."

"No, but there's a meadow that's great for picnics. On a clear day, you can see a gray castle on the cliffs."

"Okay," Johnson said with interest, her gaze focused on Mick.

"No one knows who built it," Mick went on. "But it's at least a thousand years old. Probably older. Eventually, the Lords of Velburg, this powerful family who ruled the area, took the castle. They seemingly came outta nowhere, and, a century later, they all vanished as quickly as they had appeared. While they were still in power, though, one of the lords decided he wanted to fight in the Third Crusade for Jerusalem. Now, one of the knights who went with him had recently fallen in love with a local peasant girl, and the two were betrothed. It was super rare for a peasant to marry a knight, so people in town spread the rumor that she used dark magic to enchant the knight and bind him to her. The evenin' before the lord and the knights left for the Crusade, the peasant girl had the knight swear an oath that he'd return and marry her when the fighting was over."

Mick paused the monologue, enjoying the way he drew in Johnson's eyes and attention.

"This is too perfect," Johnson said.

A bat screeched. They looked up and saw its silhouette between them and the moon.

"And we haven't even gotten to the good part," Mick replied as he lowered his head back in Johnson's direction and continued the story. "The knight took a lover before the Crusaders even reached the Holy Land. They say somewhere in the Balkans."

"Then he never returned to her...."

"Exactly. He stayed with his lover in the Balkans. Years later, when the Crusaders who survived returned here, they told the peasant girl her betrothed had been killed in battle. But she didn't believe them. She knew he'd fallen for another girl and abandoned her. Over the years, she became more and more of a hermit, and, eventually, she moved into these woods to live in solitude. Shortly after, all the remaining Lords of Velburg and their descendants disappeared."

"And you *don't* believe in a Box Witch?"

"It's a folktale. Every town in Germany has got one. Or ten."

"I think we found a new origin story for the witch," Johnson responded. "That poor girl paid quite a price for the knight's gold and glory."

Mick laughed, and a second later, a crackling noise came from the woods, just outside the open wall of the church. Johnson and Mick turned their heads in its direction.

"Did you hear that?" Johnson whispered in a panic.

Mick pointed his flashlight toward the woods.

They saw nothing except the gentle sway of the trees, the branches, and the bushes.

"I swear I heard something," Johnson whispered.

Mick stayed quiet, studying the woods.

Another crackling noise issued from the darkness. This time, louder. The two stood. Their hearts beat faster. The hair on the back of Mick's neck stood on end. Johnson felt her heart beating in her throat, and her blood grew warmer. Eyes wide, they backed toward the tower. A bush in the wood line moved. Johnson grabbed Mick as they pressed themselves against the back wall. The bush seemed to grow and change form. It lurched toward them. Johnson screamed. The being moved on them with a stunning speed. Mick dropped the flashlight and braced himself while Johnson looked for something on the ground to fight with. A moment later, a bright light shone in their faces, and they couldn't see anything.

"Get on the ground, faces in the dirt," came a stern, deep voice from behind the bright light.

In shock, neither moved.

"Get on the fucking ground!" came the raised voice again.

The two dropped to the ground with their chests and faces against the grass. The being stepped over them. Mick felt his hands grabbed, placed on the small of his back, and secured with what felt like zip ties. He turned his head to the other side to look at Johnson. Her hands were tied, too. Lying silently, they heard the being breathing over them.

"Two unidentified persons detained, sir," came the voice, this time subdued and quieter, followed by the same crackling sound.

"Roger. On my way," a voice over a radio responded.

"Guys, we're out of play. We're public affairs photographers," Johnson said, her face against the ground.

"Shut up," the man standing over them replied harshly.

All the fear in Johnson's heart now turned to anger. She hated being told what to do, especially when she knew she was right. She looked at Murphy. He was quiet.

"Scouts," she whispered.

Mick nodded his head.

"They think we're in play," he said. "We're fucked."

A moment later, they heard someone walking toward them. Johnson turned her head to the side and strained to catch a glimpse, her face still pressed in dirt. Two shadowy figures, one tall and skinny and the other normally proportioned, approached the man standing over them, whom she now saw to be wearing a highly-camouflaged ghillie suit.

"Don't look at us," the man above them said, pointing his flashlight directly in her face.

"Asshole," she mumbled.

"What are we gonna do with them, sir?" the man asked one of the individuals who had joined him. "Think they're OPFOR?"

"They don't look like they're dressed for OPFOR. And why would they be out here?" the officer said to the man. "I'm not sure who they are."

"We're not OPFOR," Johnson said, exasperated. "We're public affairs. We are totally out of play. We were out here to photograph the attack your company is planning tonight."

"I know our public affairs photography guy, sir," said the man. "Neither of these two are photographers."

"No, no, we're not your brigade's public affairs. We didn't come up here from Italy with you guys. We're stationed here, in Hohenfels. We're from a different public affairs office."

"You're stationed in Hohenfels?" asked the officer.

"Yes, sir. We are," Johnson replied. "But we're not opposing force. We're out of play."

"But if you're stationed here, I'm sure you know a lot of soldiers in the OPFOR, don't you?" asked the officer.

Mick laughed under his breath.

"Yes, sir," she replied disdainfully. "But that has nothing to do with this. I'm not going to inform them of your position."

The officer approached Johnson and knelt down to speak with her more politely.

"Listen, I believe you," he said gently. "But, unfortunately, we can't take the risk you two are OPFOR spies posing as public affairs. I'm sure you know what scouts do, don't you?"

"Yes. I know, sir."

"Then you know we can't risk our position getting leaked to OPFOR. The entire company's attack would be jeopardized."

Johnson sighed.

"I'm sorry," said the officer. "We'll let you two go in the morning. For tonight, we'll need to bring you to our forward operating base."

The officer stood up and walked back to the man who'd originally detained Johnson and Mick. He spoke to the ghillie-suited soldier in a low voice, instructing him what to do with their detainees.

Johnson turned her face toward Mick. He was still quiet, taking account of his surroundings.

"I wonder where their FOB is," Mick whispered to Johnson.

"Outside of Panzer. They just moved it."

"Good. Not too far."

Straining to look at each other while their faces were pressed against the ground, Johnson and Mick waited for their captors' next move. After a few moments, they heard the officer tell the ghillie-suited man goodbye and then walk away. The ghillie-suited man helped them both to their feet and led them out of the chapel, their hands still restrained behind their backs. He walked them toward the dirt road, past their van and down the trail for what seemed like half a mile until they reached an idling Humvee with a driver waiting outside the vehicle. The man set them in the back seats of the Humvee and blindfolded them with bandanas. He told the driver what to do with them and then departed in a hurry.

Blindfolded in the back seat of a Humvee and alone with a driver who refused to speak with them, both Johnson and Mick were nervous. When the vehicle stopped after a short drive, the doors opened, and they were led through the entrance of a large drash tent. Through their bandanas they could tell the drash was lit with dim, red light bulbs, meant to cut down on light pollution and help conceal the position of the forward operating base. They could make out several other voices in the room with them. Suddenly, their bandanas were ripped from their faces, and they found themselves standing in front of a long table against the side of the drash. Four soldiers surrounded them.

"We're about to cut the zip ties," one of the soldiers said. "When we do, we need you to empty your pockets. You'll be searched afterward. If anything is found on your person, you will be in violation of the rules and regulations that oversee fair play of this exercise, as stated in JMRC's policy letter 47-94, and are liable to be punished under the Uniform Code of Military Justice. Do you understand?"

"Dude, we're out of play," Johnson snapped. "What don't you guys get about that?"

"No one is out of play in the Box," replied a solider from behind them.

When their restraints were cut, they emptied their pockets, and one of the soldiers led the pair through the back door of the drash into another chamber with several cots, blankets, and MREs.

"You could be in here for a while," the soldier who led them into the room said. "I'd make myself comfortable if I were you."

"Thanks," Johnson replied with apathy as she made her way to a cot.

"Latrines are outside," the soldier continued. "If you need to use them, let one of us know. If you try to escape from here, you'll be in violation of the rules and—"

"And regulations of the JMRC policy letter number whatever," Johnson quickly interrupted. "We get it. Thanks."

The soldier stared at her.

"You better start taking this seriously, specialist," he sneered. "You could find yourself in a lot of trouble."

Johnson held her hands above her head and raised her eyebrows.

"Not in play," she said sarcastically.

After the soldier left, Johnson and Mick sat down on cots, facing each other.

"Mick, I've got to say, nothing like this has ever happened to me in the fifteen exercises I've covered in Hohenfels," said Johnson. "I mean, this is some seriously crazy shit."

"It was bound to happen eventually," he said. "We've been pretty reckless out here."

"I think if it was up to them, they'd keep us locked up in this place 'til the end of the exercise in two weeks. But it won't take long for Major Byrne to realize we're gone in the morning. I'm sure we'll be out of here before noon."

The two locked eyes.

"Look what those cylinders of yours have gotten us into, Mick," she said with a soft smile.

Laying down on the cot, Mick closed his eyes. He almost immediately began drifting in and out of sleep. All of Mick's surroundings in the small room in the back of the drash melted into a dreamscape surrounded by oscillating magentas and yellows that danced around the room like a haywire pinball in his mind's eye. He straddled two realties in which the laws of nature itself and everything he understood about the world was negotiable. And there was Johnson. Sitting on the cot across from his, she became an active participant in the breaking down and manipulation of the new laws. He saw the two of them being led out of the chapel, making their way through the dense forest toward the road. He watched as the doors to the Humvee were opened and the two of them were placed inside and blindfolded. He followed the vehicle as it drove through the Box toward the east side, past the grey castle on the cliff, through a grove of trees, and across a bridge that spanned a river. And then he saw her, sitting there on the cot across from his, calling his name.

"Mick, Mick! Get up! Let's get out of here!"

He blinked open his eyes.

What was real?

"Mick, come on! Major Byrne is here!" Johnson said to him.

He sprang up.

"What time is it?" he asked.

"Late," Johnson replied. "Or early. I don't know! But let's go!"

Mick followed Johnson through the tent doors that led to the larger chamber where they had left their belongings on the table. Major Byrne was there. They greeted him and grabbed their things. Leaving the tent, Byrne stopped and turned back to one of the privates on guard duty in the room.

"Just so I can ensure something like this doesn't happen again, can I get the names of the individuals who detained my soldiers, please?" he asked.

The soldiers in the room snapped to the position of attention.

"Yes, sir," one of the privates replied. "That was Lieutenant Clark and Staff Sergeant Killian."

"Thanks," replied Major Byrne, turning to leave.

"Wait, sir," Johnson spoke up. "There was a third person there when we were detained."

Major Byrne looked at the private, who wore a confused expression.

"There were only two people who detained you, specialist. I assure you. The guys here have been talking about it all morning."

"Are you trying to protect someone, private?" asked Major Byrne. "Because if you are, I promise this will not turn out well for you."

"Sir, with all due respect, I am not trying to protect anyone," he said anxiously. "A third person drove them back to the FOB, but only two were involved in the arrest."

Major Byrne turned to Johnson and Mick, whose bewildered faces perfectly mirrored one another.

"You two must have been seeing things," he told them.

Following Major Byrne to his car, the two were dumbfounded. They quietly opened the doors and took seats in the back, staring at each other. Major Byrne turned on some music and took off down the road and over a bridge that crossed a river. Mick looked out the window, straining to remember why this river and the trip across it seemed so familiar.

Was it a distant dream?

As the car emerged from a densely forested grove in the middle of changing to the colors of autumn, a cliff appeared in the distance. Mick squinted his eyes.

He recognized his surroundings, and in a moment of hazy fear, he knew exactly where he was.

"The grey castle...," he whispered to himself. "But how have we come so far?"

Go the Spoils

Forest of Dry Bones

"...Our bones are dried up, and our hope has perished. We are cut off completely."

— Ezekiel 37:11

In the north of France lies a region of the country roughly the size of the small state of Massachusetts. Its terrain is marked by farmlands and rolling hills, occasionally punctuated by vast, unpopulated forests. But these topographical features are not what make this place remarkable. Instead, it is what happened here in the middle of the previous century that serves to set this region apart from its neighbors and why the annals of history will forever remember its name.

To appreciate this story, one must first understand that just north of these farms, forests, and hills, in the northernmost counties of this northern region, a string of beaches and cliffs abut the famous English Channel, which, in the days of Hitler and the Third Reich, served as a massive, twenty-mile-wide moat, separating the Allies from the Axis.

It was on these beaches and cliffs that one of the largest and most daring seaside invasions in the history of the planet took place, giving the Allies a foot in the door to Hitler's "Fortress Europe." The successful invasion secured a point through which millions of U.S., British, and Canadian troops were funneled and surged toward the Nazi capital of Berlin.

By now, it must be clear the region in question is that of Normandy. But it is not the D-Day invasions that mark the beginning of this story, but events slightly earlier, in the two years that preceded June 6th, 1944, during which General Rommel worked feverishly to fortify the coastline of Europe, hastily constructing myriad concrete structures in preparation for the anticipated Allied invasion.

No one knows the precise number of bunkers built in Normandy during that time, but estimates run in the tens of thousands. It is clear the Germans allocated a tremendous amount of resources to the protection of the coast and inland areas, though they were never certain where the Allies would choose to invade. This story centers on one of those concrete bunkers, a mushroom bunker, as the particular type has since been called. Built in 1942 to accompany novel radar equipment and a team of operators, the bunker was placed on the property of the Dubois family in a forest near their home, about thirty kilometers south of the coastline.

The Dubois had always been a respected family in the area. The father, Monsieur Dubois, was the inheritor of an apple orchard and a small company that produced a highly sought-after brand of *calvados*, an apple brandy specific to the region. He kept long hours, doing much of the harvesting of the crop, pressing and distilling of the cider, and bottling of the product himself. The orchard sat opposite the previously mentioned forest, on the east side of the family home, a modest, centuries-old château built of brown granite. The front-facing windows were framed in white brick, which Madame Dubois kept meticulously clean, as she appreciated the striking contrast between the bright brick and the dark granite. The main section of the home had two stories, with a small, square tower on each side, both of them rising toward their respective conical peaks, creating a perfectly symmetrical, triple-pinnacled example of Châteauesque architecture reminiscent of the French Renaissance at its finest.

In this home lived Monsieur Dubois, his wife, their two young children, and a housekeeper. Their children, a boy and a girl, were named Gerard and Vivienne. And they were twins.

Owing to the rural nature of the family property, Gerard and Vivienne were largely cut off from other kids their age. And while they didn't have an extensive group of neighborhood children to play with, they did have each other. At all hours of the day, they could be found running through the apple orchard or exploring the forest, either defending the realm from invading Viking barbarians, Gerard's favorite pastime, or searching for the lost ruins of ancient kingdoms, Vivienne's favorite pastime. Of course, the twins never discovered any ruins in their small forest, except for one coin mysteriously found in the topsoil. It was a *denarius*, minted in the ninth century, bearing the image of Emperor Louis the Pious, son of Charlemagne. After Vivienne pulled it from the earth, she dashed back to the house and watched, alongside her brother, while the ancient emperor grew more and more visible as the dirt dissolved under the cold, running water.

Vivienne carried the coin with her everywhere she went. She had always wanted to be an archaeologist, and, after that day, she was even more convinced. Even at the young age of seven, she began asking her parents for books about the Carolingian Empire so she could identify the coin she'd excavated. Though the bookstores in Normandy didn't have much of a selection (especially after 1940, with the worker shortages), Monsieur Dubois would take occasional trips to Paris to distribute his *calvados* among the shops that sold his product. Whenever he traveled there, he was diligent to return to his family with gifts, and, after the "coin incident," or "*l'incident de la pièce,*" as it became known among the family, he always returned to his daughter with a book.

Equipped with newly-acquired knowledge of professional archaeology, Vivienne devised a plan to survey the entire property for additional traces of the once-glorious empire. Gerard, for his part, loved following his sister around and helping her with the surveys and excavations. Although he didn't share her passion for archaeology, he did have a passion for digging in the dirt. And his sister would return the favor by helping him fend off the barbarians, so long as they'd finished surveying the day's designated plot of land.

With such a schedule, it was common for the pair of twins to be late to their family dinner, forcing Monsieur Dubois to leave his wife at the dining table and venture into the woods to find his children. However annoying the routine searches were, he never disciplined them for being late. Not even once. On the contrary, Monsieur Dubois and his wife were grateful the pair got along so well, and they were always careful to safeguard the relationship between their two children, knowing that, unlike the kids who lived nearer to town, all the twins had in this world was each other.

Gerard and Vivienne adored one another, and they had as beautiful a childhood as one could hope for. That is, until the spring of 1942, when their forest was chosen for the previously mentioned radar installation and the concrete bunker. No longer were the children allowed to play in the woods, and, even worse for them, their parents forbade them from leaving the house without one of the adults by their side. They were, after that point, prisoners in their home.

Over the course of several weeks, the twins watched with saddened eyes from the windows of the château as a team of Nazi engineers laid the foundations of a bunker and constructed radar equipment on the boundary of their beloved forest. Trees were taken down, concrete was poured, and, when the project was finally complete, an ugly, grey monstrosity protruded from the wood line, and a radar tower extended high above the second floor of the Dubois home.

As the months dragged on, the Dubois family learned to live alongside the team of Nazi radar operators. Monsieur and Madame Dubois maintained a hope that one day the Allies would liberate the country, or perhaps the war would come to an end and the Nazis would de-militarize their region. But that seemed an unlikely outcome. (Their radios had been confiscated at the beginning of the occupation years ago, so there was no way for them to know how the war was progressing.) It was best, they decided, to accept the reality of the present situation and plan to make the best of it.

In accordance with their plan, Madame Dubois continued schooling her children, doing her best to keep feeding the flame of Vivienne's love of the humanities and trying to distract them both from the goings-on of the Nazi bunker just outside their home, which, as the entire family noticed in the first months of the summer of 1944, became busier and busier, until that fateful day in the first week of June, when everything changed.

***

After running a hand through his short, gray hair, an aged Gerard brought a shaky cup of tea to his mouth for a sip. The sun shone on his wrinkled face as he stood next to the window of the kitchen in the old château. He stared out at the forest, waiting for an update from his granddaughter. Hearing the front door open, he turned toward the entrance of the kitchen and listened as a set of footsteps in the hallway drew nearer.

"Vivienne, *as-tu trouvé quelque chose?*" he questioned, asking a young woman rounding the corner of the kitchen and walking toward him if she'd found anything in the woods today.

The young woman placed a metal detector in the corner between a pantry and the wall and then turned toward the old man and smiled sincerely. Her denim overalls were covered in dirt. She had a small, heart-shaped face and wore her blonde hair in a ponytail. As she approached the old man, her grandfather, she threw her arms around his neck and kissed him on the cheek, telling him she had not found anything today, but that she would, soon, and that it was only a matter of time before they discovered what they were looking for.

"*C'est inévitable,*" she said.

Sighing, the man walked with difficulty from the window to a small kitchen table, pulled out a chair, and heavily plopped himself into it. He lowered his head into his tired, shaking hands. About one month prior, something had come over him. He had become obsessed, asking his granddaughter to come to the château and do what he physically could not. Originally, he thought it would be an easy task, but the lack of any progress over the past month had dawned in him the idea that they might not be successful. He had become terribly anxious about it, and the anxiety now fueled whatever ailed him. His shaking grew worse, and the more he shook, the less time he thought he had. And the less time he thought he had, the more guilt he felt for not starting the project earlier. It had become an awful cycle, and, although she tried, his granddaughter Vivienne could only do so much to slow the rate at which his ailment advanced and his worries increased.

All that changed, however, the very next morning when Vivienne did find what they were looking for. Calls were made to the proper authorities, and plans to carry out an excavation on the Dubois property forest quickly set into motion.

***

One of the calls made in the aftermath of the discovery, in reference to the safety of the upcoming excavation, was made to the office of a certain Colonel Henry Anderson, an officer with the U.S. Army stationed at a base in Germany. Unmarried and childless, the colonel had made the military a career and spent much of the previous decade working within what is known as U.S. Army Europe.

"This is Colonel Anderson," the American uttered as he picked up the ringing telephone in his office.

"Henry, how the hell are ya'?" came a deep voice from the other side of the line.

The colonel looked down at the caller ID panel, and instantly his eyes grew large.

"Sir," he blurted, "I'm sorry. I hadn't checked the caller ID until just now."

"What are you doing?"

"Right now, sir? Just addressing some last-minute items before the weekend," Henry replied.

"You have a lot on your plate next week?"

"A fair amount, sir. Why do you ask?"

"You'll have to delegate those responsibilities to someone else. I'm sending you to France."

"France, sir? What's going on there?"

"Some archaeologists up in Normandy think they found a couple of our boys."

"Our boys, sir? As in soldiers from D-Day?" Henry questioned.

"That's right," replied the deep voice. "Every few years, they dig up some D-Day stuff. And, with the possibility of unexploded ordinance, we don't let the excavators take any risks without someone there who knows what all that shit looks like."

"Of course, sir."

"I know you miss working in explosive ordinance disposal, so I figured you were the right man for the job."

"Thank you, sir. And you're right; I miss it."

"This won't look like the explosives you dealt with in Iraq, but it'll scratch the itch. If you do come across something, we'll bring in a civilian bomb squad team or dispatch support from our EOD guys down in Italy. I want you there as a set of eyes, Henry. Nothing more."

"Yes, sir."

"You'll be running point for us on this. Even with the non-EOD issues. There will be a couple civilian guys there from the Defense POW/MIA Accounting Agency. If they can confirm the bodies are American, you'll need to make arrangements with the Honor Guard folks over at Stuttgart. They'll help you set up a funeral and get the remains moved to one of our cemeteries in Normandy. You'll be reporting directly to me on this. If you need anything, don't be afraid to reach out."

"Roger, sir."

"Oh, and Henry?"

"Yes, sir?"

"If memory serves, you're a real nerd about World War Two, aren't you?"

"I wouldn't call myself a nerd, sir, but I do love the Second World War," Henry responded.

"Good. Have fun up there," came the voice through the phone, just before the line cut out.

***

Departing from his house in Vilseck, Germany, Colonel Henry Anderson arrived at the château, thirty kilometers south of the coastline of Normandy the afternoon of the following Monday. He parked his car in the horseshoe driveway just outside the front door. Hearty vines had long ago overtaken the facade of the home, and the white bricks that had once been so carefully maintained had since turned a gloomy shade of gray, perfectly matching the color of the sky on the day the colonel arrived. He glanced at the dark forest to his right as he approached the door. After a quick knock, the door opened, and the colonel was greeted by young Vivienne, who welcomed him into the château.

"You are Colonel Anderson of the U.S. Army?" she asked as he passed through the doorframe.

"Please, call me Henry," he replied, setting his luggage on the floor and extending his arm for a handshake.

The entryway was tight. Henry could see what he thought was a dining room at the end of the hallway, near the back of the house. The kitchen extended from the right and a flight of stairs from the left.

"Thank you for coming on such short notice, Henry. We are all very eager to begin the excavation in the morning."

"Orders are orders," he stated.

Vivienne tilted her head to the side.

"Not that I'm not happy to be here," he said enthusiastically, trying to backpedal after realizing how negative his comment sounded. "Quite the opposite, actually. I couldn't have asked for a better assignment. Had a lot of paperwork I was supposed to do this week, but this gave me an excuse to offload that onto someone else."

He looked at Vivienne. There was a brief pause.

"And I'm big into World War Two history," he continued. "Love it, actually. This mission is right up my alley."

"I am glad to hear that, Henry. I hope our little excavation can be rewarding for you. May I show you to your room?"

As she asked this, Gerard descended the stairs and crossed the entryway, slowly making his way toward the kitchen.

"Is this your grandfather?" Henry asked. "The owner of the estate?"

"Yes, this is Gerard," she replied, smiling in her grandfather's direction.

"Thank you for letting me stay in your home, sir," Henry said in a raised voice toward the old man.

Gerard stopped in his tracks and looked over at his granddaughter and the colonel, staring.

"I'm Henry Anderson," the colonel continued. "Looking forward to being part of the excavation."

After a second or two of inspecting Henry up and down, Gerard continued his difficult journey to the kitchen without saying a word.

Henry turned his face toward Vivienne, a slightly puzzled expression in his eyes.

"He does not speak English," she said. "And he has not been feeling well lately, so please don't take that personally."

"No offense taken," Henry replied, shrugging off the awkward exchange.

Henry followed Vivienne up the stairs and down a hallway to a bedroom that had been prepared for the guest. She explained where the bathroom was, how to work the light switches, and that if he wanted to take a walk to the excavation site, she would be happy to show him in about one hour, an offer he eagerly accepted.

After Vivienne left, he set his duffel bag on the bed and hung his suit carrier in the walk-in closet, where he saw dozens, if not hundreds, of old, glass bottles with disintegrating labels. He walked to the edge of the room and pulled open the blinds, revealing the apple orchard on a hill to the side of the house. Henry couldn't tell if the apple trees were withered and dying, or if it was simply the end of the season, when the trees finish bearing fruit for the year. Regardless, the grove appeared sad, aging, and exhausted, as if no one had cared for it in many years.

Around an hour later, Henry took a tan blazer from the suit carrier and put it on over his brown sweater. Walking down the stairs, he found Vivienne helping her grandfather eat dinner in the kitchen.

"Are you hungry?" she asked, seeing the colonel enter.

"Not really," he replied, placing his hand over his stomach. "I stopped for food a couple times on the way here. I'm probably good for the night."

"As you wish," she said. "Feel free to snack on anything you find in the kitchen while you are here. Are you ready to see the excavation site?"

"Very," he said.

When Vivienne finished helping Gerard, she took a light windbreaker from the entryway closet, and the two left through the front door and made their way to the wood line.

Just before they got to the forest, Henry noticed something in the woods and stopped walking.

"What the hell is that?" he asked, looking at a concrete structure roughly the shape of a mushroom.

It was covered with vegetation, and the trunk of a tree had grown through the foundation on its back side, splitting a large piece of concrete in two. It looked as if the forest itself was reclaiming its territory from the man-made imposition.

"That... is... a Nazi bunker," Vivienne responded slowly, staying where she was at the edge of the woods as Henry approached the bunker.

"You're kidding me," he said as he reached out and touched it. "Right here on your family's property. Can we go inside?"

"No one has stepped foot inside that bunker in...," she said as she added up the years in her mind, "maybe sixteen or seventeen years?"

"That's oddly specific."

"It was me. I am the last person who went inside that bunker. When my grandfather found out, he was furious and made me promise never to go inside again."

"Why did he react like that?"

"Bad memories, I guess," she said. "But once he made me promise not to go back inside, it quickly became the only thing I wanted to do."

"But you obeyed his orders."

"I did," she said introspectively. "And it's probably why I became an archaeologist."

"Wait, you're an archaeologist?"

"Of course. I thought you knew this."

"That was not communicated to me in the emails I was forwarded," Henry responded.

"How did you think the graves were discovered?" she asked.

"I assumed the bones had been unearthed from someone tilling a piece of land or putting in a new barn or something. I figured the archaeologists were brought in afterward to confirm the findings and prepare the excavation."

"No, it was not so incidental."

"How *did* you locate the graves, then?"

"I often walk these woods with a metal detector," she replied. "Sometimes searching for a find, sometimes to relax."

She walked up to the bunker and stood next to Henry. Bringing her face very near the concrete, as if to gaze upon some fine detail or chip in the surface, she reached out her hand and ran her finger across the bunker.

"Forbidden rooms with hidden secrets and buried Nazi treasure," she said, turning to Henry. "All very captivating for a young mind, don't you think?"

"No doubt," he said. "It's no wonder you were drawn to archaeology."

She smiled softly.

"Maybe it was my grandfather's plan all along," she said.

"What do you mean?"

"He was also an archaeologist. For many years, he was one of France's most famous experts on Charlemagne and the Carolingians."

"Is everyone in Normandy an archaeologist?" Henry asked with a chuckle.

Vivienne laughed.

"No," she said. "There really are not many of us. My grandfather tried to get my father interested in archaeology, but that endeavor was not successful. Instead, my father went into business. Then, when I came into the world, my grandfather did all he could to get me into archaeology."

"And it worked."

"It did," she said, nodding. "It worked."

Looking out into the forest, she gestured in the direction of the excavation site.

"Come on," she continued. "Let's check out the graves."

The two made their way into the forest. It was not terribly dense, but the overcast nature of autumn in Normandy and the thick, full leaves of the trees made the area where they walked exceptionally dark.

They walked for several minutes until they came to an open space among the woods. One large tree extended high above the rest, with a trunk nearly twice the size of the others there. Vivienne pointed to the base of the tree.

"Here," she said. "This is where we'll excavate tomorrow."

A series of short poles stuck in the ground, cordoning the border of a space roughly two meters by three meters.

Henry looked confused.

"This is it?" he asked. "No preliminary digging has been started? How do you even know this is a grave? The metal detector could have been picking up anything."

"No," Vivienne replied, "there is not much in these woods for the metal detector to pick up. And to confirm, I borrowed a GPR from my lab and ran it over the site. There are definitely graves here."

"GPR?" Henry asked.

"Sorry. Ground penetrating radar. It is like a lawnmower," she said, holding out her hands as if she was mowing. "Except this machine has a radar system that feeds data onto an HD screen in real time."

"And the radar identified bones here?"

"GPR cannot locate bones," she replied. "But it can show where the ground has been disturbed. The entire area was shoveled out and re-filled. At least enough space for two adults. Maybe more."

Henry lowered his face and gazed at the suspected gravesite.

"Okay, then," he said. "Then there are graves here."

"It is certain."

"But what makes you think they're Americans?"

Vivienne looked away, pausing.

"Vivienne?" Henry continued.

"It is because of what my grandfather knows about what happened here, all those years ago."

Vivienne and Henry locked eyes.

"What does your grandfather know?"

"He was very young in 1944," she replied after another pause. "His memories from that day are not perfect. And his parents never spoke to him about it afterward. It was like the family pretended the invasion never happened."

"What does he remember?"

After pausing yet again, Vivianne began the story.

"He remembers a lot of bombs falling very near to them. Well, what he thought was very near to them. In reality, the closest bombing sites were ten or twelve kilometers from here.

But he thought he was going to die. He remembers the bombs coming for more than a day, just before the invasion."

"Right," Henry said. "On the 5th of June. The Allies were softening up the Germans and wiping out as many communication points as they could."

"But my grandfather did not know this. He thought the whole world was coming down around them. They stayed in the basement long after the bombing stopped, while the fate of the world was being decided in the skies and on the shores."

A small critter ran through the brush behind them. They both turned around as it ran up a tree, several meters away.

"When did these two Americans show up here? And what happened to them?" Henry asked, glancing at the graves again.

"They were airborne paratroopers," Vivienne said solemnly.

As she spoke, Henry realized what must have occurred.

"They missed their targets," he added.

"Yes," she replied. "As I am sure you know, the paratroopers were the first soldiers to land in Normandy. Hours before the others took the beaches."

"They dropped behind German lines," he commented. "They were supposed to take roads and bridges and make it easier for the ground forces to push deeper into Normandy after the beachhead."

"But because of dense fog and heavy firing from the Germans, many of the planes dropped their paratroopers very far from where they were supposed to," she said.

"So these poor souls parachuted into your family's forest, and I'm guessing the bunker back there had something to do with why they didn't see the end of the war?" he asked as he looked back in the direction of the concrete structure.

"Precisely," she replied. "My grandfather says that while they were in the basement, he and the family heard several short bursts of machine gun fire and could tell it was very close. Just above their heads. Later that day, when they came outside for the first time, they found the lifeless bodies of the two Americans lying in the grass."

"These guys must have walked into a trap," Henry said.

"I think so," Vivienne agreed. "It is very likely the Nazis saw them descending from the sky. All the Nazis had to do was sit behind one of the machine guns and wait for them to walk out of the woods."

"Poor guys probably never saw it coming. What a terrible way to go."

"Yes," she said, nodding her head.

"How do you think they ended up buried out here? The Nazis do it?"

"No, the Nazis did not bury these men," Vivienne replied. "They made my grandfather's father do it. At least this is what he told me. He was not allowed to accompany his father during the burial, and the family never came into the woods again after that point, so he did not know where to look in the decades after the war, when the Americans were trying to recover the missing."

"How long did it take for the Allies to get here?"

"I believe it was three or four weeks. The Nazis abandoned this bunker a little over two weeks after the invasion. The Allies arrived shortly after."

"I hope we can identify these men," Henry said. "It will be easier because they were paratroopers. That narrows down the list."

"But still hundreds, I think, no?"

"I'm not sure. The team from the DPAA will have a better idea."

The forest had grown darker. Henry and Vivienne walked back toward the château, possibly along the same path the American paratroopers took just before their deaths. A light fog moved in. Exiting the forest, Henry took another look at the bunker, shrouded in darkness and mist. For nearly seventy-five years, it had quietly stalked the château from the edge of the woods—watching, haunting the Dubois family.

What curses had it inflicted on them? he thought.

There was a light on in the kitchen of the home. Its warm luminescence spilled into the yard from the window through which Gerard peered, waiting for his granddaughter to return from her excursion into the forest.

"Come on," Vivienne said to Henry. "Let's go inside."

***

The next morning came slowly for the colonel. He rolled around and readjusted the sheets in the bed of the room above the apple orchard for what seemed to him the entirety of the night. He couldn't get the image out of his mind of paratroopers walking out of the woods and being gunned down without warning.

It wasn't that these soldiers' deaths were particularly gruesome, relative to other tragedies happening that day. Rather, it was the connection he felt as a witness, of sorts, to the last moments of their lives that kept him awake that night. Their families grew old and died and received no answers about what happened to them. Nor were the families allowed the solace of knowing the remains of the one they loved were rescued from the foreign land of nightmare and brought to a place of peace. Their resting places had been forgotten; the young soldiers were cut off, lost. Until now. And, as one of the few people with access to what they left behind, he felt as if he'd inherited such precious information, a window into a few secret hours of the D-Day invasions. The only place anyone could *read* about what happened to these soldiers was right there in the dirt, under the big tree in the forest. And he knew that with this privilege came a unique responsibility.

That morning, just before getting in the shower, he grabbed a journal out of his bag and jotted down a couple thoughts:

There is a museum in these Norman woods. It hosts a single lonely exhibit, and I am its only guest.

Walking down the stairs after showering and putting on a fresh set of clothes, Henry heard something in the driveway. He turned the corner and peered through the small window by the door. A shiny, black cargo van had pulled in and parked behind his car. The doors opened, and out stepped two men and a woman.

"Good morning," he heard from behind.

Henry turned around to see Vivienne standing in the entryway.

"My colleagues have arrived," she said as she gestured toward the door. "May I introduce you?"

They walked outside and found the three individuals unloading equipment from the back of the van.

"*Bonjour,* Vivienne," the woman said, leaning forward to kiss Vivienne on the cheek.

"Hello, everyone," she replied. "Is it okay if we all speak English for Colonel Anderson? He's here from the U.S. Army to oversee the excavation and make sure we don't blow ourselves up."

There was quiet laughter among the group.

"Of course we can," one of the men happily interjected in an accent that was certainly not French.

The colonel looked his way.

"Oh, you're an American?" Henry asked.

"Canadian," the man replied. "I've been working in Normandy for about seven years, but my French still isn't quite perfect, as my friends here love to point out."

He shot a playful look toward Vivienne and the woman standing next to her.

The Canadian wore a checkered shirt tucked into blue jeans. This excavation was clearly not the first for either article of clothing. The same could be said for the attire of everyone standing around the van, except for Colonel Anderson, who looked clean and dapper, as was normal for him whenever the situation allowed.

"This is Mark," Vivienne said, pointing in the Canadian's direction. "He specializes in the excavation of World War Two-era sites."

She then turned toward the woman standing next to her.

"And this is Claudia. She is brand new to our research facility. Graduated from university only last year."

Claudia smiled shyly at Henry. She had curly, shoulder-length hair and wore earrings shaped like tiny shovels.

"And this is Pierre," Vivienne concluded, looking at the oldest among the group of archaeologists. "He is our bioarchaeologist."

"Which means?" Henry asked.

"I specialize in the excavation of bones," Pierre chimed in.

He wore horn-rimmed glasses and had a thick, dark beard with streaks of white. Its length far surpassed the hair on his head, which he kept short to hide his receding hairline.

After the introductions, the team gathered the rest of the boxes and equipment and followed Vivienne from the château to the wood line.

As the team passed the concrete structure sitting menacingly on the edge of the forest, Mark slowed down and gradually came to a stop.

"Vivienne?" Mark asked, looking at her from the corner of his eye. "What is this?"

Henry and Vivienne exchanged glances as the group gathered around Mark.

"That is a Nazi bunker, Mark," she responded.

"You never told us there was a bunker on your family's property! Why haven't we excavated and catalogued it?"

"My grandfather would never allow it."

"Why?"

"He doesn't want anyone going in there," she said. "And he is not fond of having people near the house who are not family."

"If it's been untouched for so long, we'd likely find artifacts *in situ*. Wasn't your grandpa an archaeologist?"

"*In situ?*" Henry asked.

"It's Latin for 'in place,'" Claudia eagerly added. "It's what we say when we find artifacts that have not been disturbed since they were last put down by the people who originally used them."

Henry thanked Claudia with a nod. She smiled and looked away.

"He is from a different generation of academics," Vivienne said kindly, but sadly, to Mark. "He hardly recognizes our niche as archaeology. Says that the Second World War is a field of study for historians, not archaeologists."

"Pity," Mark said.

Gazing at the bunker for a few moments, the team picked up the equipment again and continued their slow walk into the forest.

"Vivienne?" Pierre spoke up from the back of the group. "Is your grandfather okay with us excavating the gravesite?"

"He is," she said. "He does not see what we're doing as an excavation, but as an act of respect to the dead."

After a pleasant walk of dodging and ducking branches, they arrived at the gravesite in the forest. They set down the equipment, and Vivienne showed the crew the short poles in the ground that indicated where a hole had been dug and filled in over seven decades prior.

Mark took out a digital camera from one of the boxes and took a couple photos of the ground, the markers, and wide shots of the whole scene beneath the large tree.

Vivienne and Pierre each grabbed a trowel, which, unlike a simple shovel scoop, displayed sharp angles, a head shaped like a triangle, and a handle bearing the name "Ministére de la Culture." They bent down to their knees, on opposite sides of the marked area, with a plan to work inward toward one another.

Pierre looked at Vivienne.

"Alright," he said. "Just like we did last year in Caen. If you come across something like a bone, stop right away."

Extending her right arm forward toward the top edge of the grave, Vivienne placed the long side of the triangular tool's head against the ground and began raking a thin layer of topsoil back in her direction, accumulating a small pile of dirt by her knees after several repetitions of the same motion.

Mark put down the camera and picked up a large, plastic bucket and a shovel. As Vivienne and Pierre's piles of dirt rose, they each leaned back in turn and allowed Mark to shovel the soil into the bucket, which he then brought to Claudia, who sifted through the dirt with a tray, looking for any small artifacts that might have slipped past Vivienne and Pierre.

This cycle of collecting dirt, shoveling it into buckets, and passing it through a sifter continued for about an hour and a half, at which point arms were tired and roles were swapped. A vigilant Henry kept watch for any traces of unexploded ordinance as the excavated hole grew deeper. Another hour went by, and roles were swapped again.

"Guys," Claudia said urgently, sitting by the buckets with a sifter in her hands. "I found something."

The team converged on Claudia. She held a small, metal button in her palm.

"Looks like a button from the old army jackets the Americans wore," Mark said.

"That's exactly what it is," Henry added, glancing at Mark.

"Our first find," Pierre said. "Bag it up and label it."

Claudia reached for a small, plastic bag and dropped the dirty button inside, adding the date, the location of the excavation, a description of the object, and a code that clarified it had been found while sifting (meaning the precise place it was pulled from within the excavated area was unknown).

The team took a short break to eat the bagged lunches they'd brought to the forest. When they finished, they all returned to the tasks they were engaged in before Claudia found the button, but, after only a minute or two, Mark's trowel scraped against something hard in the soil.

"Pierre," he said as he sat back on his heels, his knees in the dirt, "I believe I've come across some bone."

Pierre walked to Mark and bent down. Using his trowel, he gently moved the dirt away from the object, revealing a bone-like surface stained with age and the brown dirt of the ground.

"Yes, this is bone," Pierre said. "We have made contact with a skeleton. Everyone, proceed carefully."

A box of smaller, more precise tools was opened, and, over the course of the next three hours, the team dragged out such an amount of dirt that the excavated area was slightly more than one meter deeper than the surface level of the ground around it.

And right in the center of the hole lay two complete skeletons.

One was taller than the other by nearly fifteen centimeters, but they were clearly both adults, and Pierre had already confirmed they were males. The team also recovered thirteen buttons, two belt clasps, a canteen, and two pairs of decomposing boots (still on the feet of the soldiers), but, much to the disappointment of Henry and the others, no dog tags on either skeleton.

As for the bones themselves, the excavators exposed them to nearly three quarters depth, enough to accurately assess what was present without dislodging the skeletons from the ground.

Pierre took a piece of paper from a binder. It displayed a highly detailed diagram of a skeleton. Using a fine-point pen, he began carefully filling in every individual bone he saw among the remains of the person lying in the dirt on the left. When he finished, he took out another sheet and did the same for the skeleton on the right.

In the meantime, Mark placed measuring rods along the sides of the grave and proceeded to take dozens of photos of the skeletons and the excavated area from every angle he could manage to achieve.

After the site had been thoroughly documented, everyone stood back and looked with pride upon their work: a perfectly excavated pit, two uncovered skeletons, and multiple bags of artifacts from this wartime grave under the big tree in the dark forest by the Dubois family château in Normandy. The team was covered in dirt from head to toe, all but Henry.

"Nicely done, everyone," Pierre said. "Two more soldiers can be laid to rest alongside their comrades."

"No dog tags, though," Henry remarked.

"The Nazis who killed these men probably took the tags off their bodies before they were put in the ground," Mark replied.

Henry agreed.

"What did you think of your first excavation?" Pierre asked, turning toward Henry.

"Considering the full extent of my archaeological knowledge came from Indiana Jones, this was much more scientific than I'd anticipated. Much more methodical."

"Yes," Pierre responded. "No swashbuckling."

"Or booby traps," Mark added, causing some laughter among the group, except from Vivienne, whose silence was now noticed.

Her eyebrows were lightly scrunched. She appeared puzzled, perplexed.

"Vivienne?" Claudia asked. "Is everything alright?"

"Yes," she said to Claudia with a soft smile. "I just thought there would be… more…."

"What do you mean?" Pierre asked.

Vivienne looked at him.

"Nothing," she replied.

"We found all we could have, Vivienne. This was everything," Pierre told her, pointing to the skeletons and the bagged artifacts. "There are more ways to identify remains than just using dog tags."

At that moment, Henry's phone buzzed.

"One of the DPAA guys just arrived," he said. "I'll head to the driveway and bring him here."

Walking back to the château, Henry saw a man with dark, ebony skin and a short, salt-and-pepper beard with glasses standing next to a car in the driveway. He held a clipboard and some notes.

"Nice to meet you, Dr. Martin," Henry said as he approached the man and introduced himself.

"Call me Randal," the doctor replied as the two shook hands.

The men made small talk as they walked through the grass en route to the dig site. Randal commented on the bunker, and Henry filled him in on the details.

"What an eyesore," Randal said.

Nearing the group, Henry prepared to introduce the forensic anthropologist to the team of archaeologists, but when they arrived at the gravesite, it became clear that Pierre already knew Dr. Randal Martin.

"Randal," Pierre said with a smile on his face. "I was hoping the agency would send you. How are you, my friend?"

"I can't complain," the doctor replied, opening his arms wide. "It's always a pleasure to be in France."

"I'm sorry our weather is not what you're used to at your lab in Hawaii. It has been a very cloudy autumn here."

"Hey, don't apologize. The wine in Normandy will more than make up for the weather," Randal said happily. "Alright, what do you have for me?"

"In terms of physical evidence, not much except the skeletons and a handful of uniform paraphernalia. But an eyewitness account suggests these individuals were paratroopers."

"Any dog tags?" Randal asked.

"Unfortunately, we did not recover any dog tags."

"Shit," he said, setting his clipboard on the ground. "Has everything been photographed?"

"Yes," Mark said.

"You're about to start lifting the bones?"

"That's right," Pierre replied.

Randal pulled a pair of surgical gloves from his pocket and walked to the excavated pit. After slipping the gloves over his hands, he laid down on his stomach at the edge of the grave and moved his face as close to the skull of the skeleton on the left as was possible without touching it. He brought forward a flashlight and aimed it through the jaw.

"We'll definitely be able to pull good dental records from this guy," Randal said as he shifted around in pursuit of the best angle from which to view the teeth.

He moved his gaze from the mouth down to the skeleton's sternum.

"Look at these cuts and fractures," he said, pointing to the breastbone.

Pierre, Mark, Vivienne, Claudia, and Henry all stepped closer and knelt down beside the grave to see what Randal was referring to.

"Machine gun fire to the chest," Randal continued.

"How terrible," Claudia said under her breath.

Randal moved toward the second skeleton and conducted the same examination.

"If these guys really were paratroopers, it shouldn't be too hard to match them to their old dental records," he said as he stood up. "It would be another story if they were regular infantry or something."

"You're confident we can find out who they were?" Henry asked.

"It'll definitely be a massive stack of records to pour over, but, if we search long enough, I'm sure we'll figure it out."

With the few hours of light that remained, the team split into two groups. Pierre and Claudia took the skeleton on the left while Vivienne and Mark took the skeleton on the right. Each team removed bone after individual bone from their respective skeletons, handing each to Henry and Randal, who carefully placed them in labeled bags and then set the bags inside a padded crate.

As the light began to fade and the last bone had been lifted, bagged, and stored, Pierre took a deep breath and wiped the sweat from his forehead.

"We are finished," he said. "Start taking the equipment back to the van. I will dump the dirt back into the pit."

***

At the château, a nervous Gerard sat in the kitchen and, despite his age and ailment, laboriously peeked out the window every few minutes. He was unsure how they still could be excavating with such dim light left in the sky. Finally, he saw someone emerge from the wood line. It was Mark, and he appeared to be carrying a heavy crate.

Gerard painstakingly watched as the crew loaded all the crates and various pieces of equipment into the van. At last, he saw his granddaughter Vivienne without anything in her arms. Instead of walking toward the driveway, she walked toward the front door.

Rushing out of the kitchen, he stared down the hallway. The knob turned, and the door opened. There stood Vivienne, tears on her cheeks. Gerard gazed at her with desperate, inquisitive eyes. She tilted her head to the side and then slowly raised her shoulders, looking at him endearingly.

Gerard made such a noise trying to choke back tears that it broke his granddaughter's heart. She ran to embrace him, and there in the hallway, resting against the wall, she stood with him and held him in his pain and his memories.

***

Walking out of the house, Vivienne approached her colleagues, who stood by the van.

"Unfortunately, my grandfather is not feeling well, so he cannot join us for dinner," she said. "But he told me we can still use the dining room and eat here if we want to."

"Is he sure?" Pierre asked. "If he is feeling ill and would prefer to have the house quiet, we can drive to town and find a tavern."

"That is kind of you, Pierre," she replied. "His bedroom is on the other side of the house, so we will not bother him."

"Very well."

The team followed Vivienne to the back of the château, where they found a shed next to the withering apple orchard. She passed around a few wet rags, which they used to wipe the smudged dirt from their hands, arms, necks, and faces. Everyone removed their shoes, and if they had outer layers they could take off, they did that as well. Then they went into the house from the back door.

The dining room table was long and rectangular. Vivienne lit candles and turned down the lights. Pierre offered Claudia the head of the table, which she accepted, with a gracious curtsy. A toast was proposed and wine glasses were immediately filled as the hungry group began eating pieces of a baguette, dipping them in a plate of seasoned olive oil.

Pierre gazed with contentment at the faces around the table. He lifted his glass in the air.

"To Claudia," he said, lowering his head so he could look at her over the top rim of his glasses. "This was your very first excavation with our lab. Not only did you find the day's first artifact, the button in the sifter that either Vivienne or I missed, but you also found the canteen and one of the belt clasps. Wonderfully done, Claudia."

Claudia's smile stretched across her face, and her cheeks gleamed red.

Pierre turned to Mark.

"Mark, our steady workhorse, our source of knowledge regarding all aspects of the Second World War. Thank you for your insight and your perspective as the foremost expert of wartime archaeology on the ground today."

Mark nodded his head and raised his glass at Pierre.

Pierre then turned to Vivienne. She was curled up and comfortable, leaning against the back of the chair, her glass of wine having already been refilled once.

"Vivienne, this excavation would not have happened without you. You made the initial discovery and brought us all here. Thank you, and well done."

She feigned a smile at him from across the table and over the flickering of a candle, but he could tell she was sad. He could see it in the way she held her lips, like she was trying to keep herself from crying.

"We love you, Vivienne."

"*Merci*, Pierre," she mouthed.

Pierre knew now was not the time to investigate what might be going on.

He turned to Randal.

"You know I always enjoy working with you, Randal. Thank you for bringing your forensic knowledge to our excavation. I am confident you will determine the identities of our soldiers."

"If the dental records exist, we'll find them," Randal responded.

"I know you will," Pierre said.

Lastly, Pierre turned to the colonel, who was the obvious outsider at the table.

Henry had greatly enjoyed the excavation, even though he didn't actually *excavate* anything. Nevertheless, he found himself wanting to accompany this group to their next excavation, and then their next, and their next, so long as they continued to work on the once-battered landscape of Normandy. It wasn't just the unique connection to the past he'd thought about that morning that captivated him; it was the joint pursuit of a noble goal that drew him in. He remembered feeling a similar way much earlier in his career, when he was younger, disposing explosives alongside a team. But this was different.

"Colonel Anderson," Pierre said with gusto. "We are still breathing. Therefore, you have succeeded in your mission."

Mark chuckled.

"I didn't have much working against me," Henry replied.

"This is true," Pierre said. "Though I believe if you did, we would be breathing even so."

He took another look around the table, his glass still raised in the air.

"To all of us," he said as everyone leaned in and tapped their glasses against his.

Vivienne got up from the table and brought out a large pot of stew she'd made the day before and re-heated on the stove.

"Vivienne, this looks incredible," Claudia said.

"I knew we would be hungry after the dig."

As the dinner commenced and empty wine bottles accumulated on the table, the conversation turned toward the previous anniversary of the D-Day invasion and how exuberant Normandy becomes every June.

"The French children run the streets with American flags painted on their faces. There are re-enactors, parachuters, old military jeeps, memorial services, great feasts, and visitors from all over the world. It really is something," Pierre said. "A celebration of liberty."

"I've always wanted to travel here for one of the anniversaries," Henry added. "But June is always a busy month for me."

"Well, you still have time," Pierre replied, cleaning his beard with a napkin. "The annual celebrations won't end anytime soon. Gratitude for the American deliverance of this continent is still very much alive. Well, at the very least, it is once per year."

"I was able to make it to the anniversary a few years ago," Randal said. "I stood on Omaha Beach and watched the sun go down across from the English Channel. It sent shivers down my spine, thinking about what happened there. The hopelessness. It was palpable. I'll never forget it."

Pierre turned to him.

"How has the search been going lately, Randal?" he asked. "Any recent victories?"

The doctor smiled.

"Last week, we brought a few Marines home who were found on the island of Roi-Namur in the Kwajalein Atoll. Horrendous fighting those boys must have gone though, judging by their remains."

"Could you identify them?" Henry asked.

"They were found with their dog tags," Randal replied, nodding.

"What does that bring the total number of missing down to?" Pierre asked. "Are you still above seventy-two thousand?"

"We've made a lot of progress these past couple years, but we haven't dropped below seventy-two just yet."

Claudia leaned forward, her elbows on the table and an inquisitive look on her face.

"What do you mean by seventy-two thousand?" she asked. "Seventy-two thousand missing soldiers?"

"Seventy-two thousand missing service members across all branches of the U.S. military," Randal responded.

Claudia's jaw dropped, and her eyes opened wide.

"Seventy-two thousand missing from America's wars! That is such an unbelievably high number!"

"No, no," Randal said. "Not from America's *wars*. That is the number of missing American service members from the Second World War *alone*."

Mark nodded slowly.

Claudia could not believe what she was hearing.

"And before I retire, I'd like to see that number drop below seventy thousand," Randal continued.

"That is a lofty goal, my friend," Pierre said.

"We owe it to them," Randal replied.

"What do we owe the dead?" Vivienne asked, looking up from the glass of wine she was holding in her lap. "They are gone. Finding them, identifying them…, it comforts us. But it does not comfort those who are dead."

"You're right," Randal replied. "They are dead. And they will never know if their remains are repatriated or if they're left to rot in a wartime grave in the mountains of some island in the Pacific."

He took a sip of his wine.

"But the society they left behind is not dead," he continued. "It lives on. In their sacrifice. In their families. In us. We don't incinerate our dead to heaps of nameless ash or toss them in mass graves like the Soviets. We bring them home, when we can, and bury them with dignity. We carve out a little piece of land and pay tribute with a gravestone. It's not much, but it's enough to tell the world they were here, they lived, and they mattered to someone. And it gives their families a place to mourn. And their families are ultimately who all this is for."

Vivienne stared past Randal.

"Family is who all this is for," she said, focusing on him.

"It is," Randal replied.

She paused, and then started.

"You know, I think you're right about that."

***

Vivienne's alarm went off at 4:45 a.m. the next morning. She jumped out of bed and got dressed in a hurry, donning a headlamp and grabbing her metal detector before flying out the door.

The dawn was dark and cold, and the bunker, which Vivienne passed on her way to the forest, looked larger and more grotesque in the absence of light. Stepping into the midst of the trees, she activated the headlamp and doubled her resolve. When she arrived at the small clearing with the big tree above the recently excavated graves, she took a deep breath and got to work.

Moving systematically across the open space, she hovered the metal detector over areas she was certain she'd already checked. Regardless, she checked them again. And then she moved to the trees that surrounded the glade. With no success, Vivienne ultimately arrived at the big tree and looked down at the freshly disturbed dirt. She stepped to the flank and peered at the back side of the large trunk, the side facing away from the clearing. There was brush and much foliage in the area around that side of the tree. She approached the shrubs and began to clear them away, enough to lower the metal detector to the forest floor. After several passes, she thought she heard a brief, quiet beep and then hovered the detector directly above the spot. A steady, loud tone emanated from the machine. Her heart began to race. She ran back to the château and immediately called Pierre.

"Pierre, *ramène l'équipe au château*," she implored, telling him to bring the team back to the property.

He objected, explaining to her, as he did the day before, that they had found everything they could have. There was nothing left in the graves to recover. Besides, he continued, the team had to clean the bones of the soldiers and prepare the skulls to be scanned for dental analysis.

Vivienne was insistent. She told him she had found something on the other side of the tree and was certain there was more to discover.

There was silence on Pierre's end, followed by a sigh.

"*D'accord*, Vivienne. *Nous y serons dans une heure*," he said, bending to her wishes.

***

Vivienne prepared breakfast for Henry and her grandfather. Originally, Henry had planned to drive to the lab and assist Randal with scouring old dental records, but Vivienne informed him that the team was on their way to the château and that another dig was about to happen. Randal would stay behind to clean the skulls and conduct the scans himself. Although Henry was curious as to how and why these plans came to be (as he thought the excavation had ended the day before), he was excited to go back into the woods and spend another day in the dirt with these people whose company he'd grown to enjoy.

The team of archaeologists arrived, and, just like the previous day, the equipment was hauled out to the big tree in the forest. A perimeter was cordoned, photos were taken, and the new excavation began.

"What do you think we are going to find here?" Claudia asked Vivienne as the two knelt side by side, dragging layers of dirt back with their trowels.

"I don't know," Vivienne replied, her stare unwavering from the ground in front of her.

"It was probably just a false signal," Claudia added. "From a low battery or something. Why would their dog tags have been buried on the other side of the tree?"

As Claudia spoke, her trowel scraped against something hard. Henry bent down to make sure she'd not made contact with unexploded ordinance. Vivienne's attention was captivated.

"Pierre," Henry said in a tone unexpectedly serious. "This looks like bone."

"Yes, this feels like bone," Claudia agreed, turning to Pierre.

Pierre rushed to the scene and pushed away some dirt. Confirming the hard object was bone, he made eye contact with Vivienne.

"There is a skeleton here," he said faintly, wide-eyed and taken aback.

The excavators continued to dig away the soil from around the skeleton. Soon, they came across a single button, full of grime and grit, which they bagged and labeled.

In the process of clearing dirt from the breastbone, Claudia commented that this skeleton displayed marks and fractures similar to the ones Randal pointed out on the remains of the paratroopers the day before, attributing them to machine gun fire.

As more of the skeleton was revealed, the team realized that something was very wrong.

"Vivienne," Pierre said, grimly, "these are the remains of a child."

Vivienne stopped digging. She leaned back and sat in the dirt, wiping her eyes and exhaling deeply.

The entire team stared at her.

"Who do these remains belong to, Vivienne?" Mark finally asked.

"This was my great-aunt," Vivienne replied, "the girl for whom I was named."

Nobody knew what to say. There was a short period of silence.

"How did your great-aunt come to be buried here, at the same tree as the American paratroopers?" Pierre asked gently.

"They died the same day," Vivienne replied, looking around at everyone.

"Your great-aunt died on D-Day?" Mark asked.

Vivienne nodded.

"How?"

"Remember I told you that my grandfather and his parents were hiding in the basement the day before the invasion, through the night, and into the next day?"

"Yes," Henry said.

"There is another piece to the story," Vivienne began. "My great-aunt was down in the basement, too. They were best friends, her and my grandfather. *Inseparable.*"

Everyone listened. The forest turned silent.

"There is a sliver of window down in the basement," she went on. "If you look from the proper angle, you can see the sky above the forest. At some point in the night, Vivienne, my grandfather's sister, started saying she had seen two men parachuting into the trees. Her parents did not believe her. They told her she was imagining it and there was no way she could have seen what she claimed. They thought it was too dark. But Gerard remembers her saying she had seen their silhouettes against a bright flash."

"That was probably anti-aircraft fire from the Germans," Mark solemnly added.

Henry nodded in agreement.

"She tried to convince her parents that she really did see two men with parachutes descending into the woods. She became convinced the soldiers were coming to liberate their cherished forest and told her father he must warn the Americans to ensure they would not walk into a German trap."

"She had it all figured out," Claudia said as she glanced at the half-excavated remains.

"When her father told her again that she was imagining what she saw, she decided to take matters into her own hands," Vivienne started again. "She waited for the right moment, when her father wasn't looking, and then ran up the stairs as fast as she could. Her father realized what she was doing and sprinted after her, followed quickly by Gerard. But they were too late. The Nazis were waiting in their machine gun nest outside the bunker. Probably very on edge. Looking for any sign of movement. When Vivienne burst through the front door, it surprised the Nazis. They swiveled the machine gun toward the house and fired on her within seconds. I doubt they even meant to do it.... Then the Americans stepped out of the woods. When they heard the firing and realized what was happening, they raised their rifles, but not fast enough. The Nazis swiveled their gun back toward the wood line and killed them, too."

Mark exhaled sharply, shaking his head and gazing at the remains.

"Why didn't you tell us about this from the start?" Henry asked.

"My grandfather carries a lot of shame because he was not able to keep his sister safe. Even after all these years, it is very difficult for him to speak of these things," Vivienne replied. "I wasn't certain we would actually find this grave, so I didn't want to share my grandfather's story if it wasn't necessary."

Pierre knelt down alongside Vivienne.

"We can take care of things from here," he said. "Tell your grandfather we have found his sister."

Vivienne stood up and grabbed the bagged button. As she walked through the woods, she thought about how to tell her grandfather of the discovery.

Exiting the forest, she looked up and saw Gerard in the window. She crossed the lawn and approached the house. Her grandfather was standing at the end of the hall when she opened the door. She held up the button inside the clear, plastic bag, and Gerard squinted to observe it. Vivienne met him at the end of the hall, where he gently took the bag from her hand and dropped the button into his palm, specks of dirt accompanying.

Gerard examined the button in detail, and then, in an instant, something clicked in the old man's mind. With every ounce of energy he had, he rushed to the kitchen, where he opened the tap and let the running water wash the dirt from the button. Gerard and Vivienne watched closely as the grit disintegrated and Emperor Louis the Pious revealed the artifact not to be a button at all, but an ancient Carolingian *denarius*.

The man's arms began to tremble. Vivienne closed the tap and helped her grandfather to his seat, where he threw his face into his hands and wept aloud.

Once he calmed down, Gerard explained to his granddaughter that his father purchased the *denarius* from an antiquarian in Paris after Vivienne had taken an interest in archaeology. Returning from the trip, their father pulled Gerard aside, gave him the coin in secret, and instructed him to bury it in the soil in a place he was sure Vivienne would dig.

And that's exactly what Gerard did on the morning of "*l'incident de la pièce.*"

***

Over the following days, Randal worked tirelessly, comparing scans of the recovered skulls to the dental records of missing D-Day paratroopers. It turned out to be quite easy. One of the soldiers had a missing molar on the right side of his mouth. Once Randal came across an X-ray with a similar anomaly, he simply looked for other similarities between the two. This led him to positively identify the first of the paratroopers. His name was Private First Class William Billings, twenty-one years old when he went missing on June 6th, 1944. He had no children and no siblings, and was survived only by his parents, who had, of course, since passed.

Regarding the second excavated soldier, Randal searched the records of everyone else on Billings' aircraft the morning of the invasion. Six paratroopers had gone missing. Four were recovered in the first decade after the war. Billings made five. That left one possible candidate, Private George Acker, whose teeth perfectly matched those of the second skeleton. Nineteen years old, he was survived by his parents and his two brothers, all of whom since passed.

***

Two fresh graves had been dug in the emerald green field of the Brittany American Cemetery in Saint-James. It was an unusually sunny and warm day in Normandy. Among a sea of white crosses and Stars of David, a small audience sat in wait at the edge of the new graves.

Colonel Henry Anderson attended in his dark blue Army Service Uniform. Dr. Randal Martin was there as well, extending his stay in Normandy just for the funeral. Pierre paid respect, as did Mark and Claudia. Various members of the cemetery staff attended, as did a handful of high-ranking officers within the organizations of both U.S. Army Europe as well as the French Armed Forces. Seven soldiers, all wearing the Army Service Uniform and holding rifles by their side, stood like statues twenty meters away.

Two funeral coaches entered the cemetery through a stone gate, drove past the chapel in slow reverence, and parked on the road nearest the fresh graves and the funeral attendees. A team of eight soldiers stepped out of the first vehicle and carried a flag-draped casket toward the graves. Those in uniform rendered salutes as the team marched forward, watching as the Honor Guard carefully positioned the casket on a temporary rack above the grave. The eight soldiers turned around and repeated the march again with the second flag-draped casket.

Service members lowered their salutes, and everyone sat down. A chaplain spoke of duty, honor, and sacrifice, and then he invited Henry to say a few words.

Henry approached the caskets, paused, and turned around to face the audience.

"It's not often that soldiers are buried in this cemetery, not anymore," he said. "I am honored to be here, witnessing this. And I offer my thanks to all who came."

He took out a handkerchief and wiped sweat from his forehead and his eyes.

"A couple days ago, when the chaplain asked if I would speak here, I didn't know what I could say. What *can* be said of the Allied invasion of Normandy that hasn't already been said by much greater men and women than I?"

He looked around at the faces in the crowd and smiled somberly at the friends he'd made over the past week.

"For that reason," he continued, "I will keep this short."

He turned to face the caskets.

"Had these soldiers been born a decade earlier or a decade later, they likely would have lived normal lives. They would have married, raised families, and punched a clock. But instead they came to Normandy, where they died as boys. And they've been lost for so long they have no friends or family to attend their funerals. But them, they're still just boys."

He took a sheet of notebook paper from his pocket, unfolded it, and read an excerpt from the address President Roosevelt delivered to the nation on the evening of the D-Day invasion:

For these men are lately drawn from the ways of peace. They fight not for the lust of conquest. They fight to end conquest.
They fight to liberate. They fight to let justice arise, and tolerance and good will among all thy people. They yearn but for the end of battle, for their return to the haven of home.
Some will never return. Embrace these, Father, and receive them, thy heroic servants, into thy kingdom.

He turned the small piece of paper over in his hands, glancing back at the caskets and wiping his face once more. After a brief pause, he faced back to the audience and lowered his head to the paper before continuing with a passage from the thirty-seventh chapter of Ezekiel:

...Thus says the Lord GOD: "Behold, I am going to open your graves and bring you up from your graves, my people....
Then you will know that I am the LORD, when I open your graves and I bring you up from your graves, my people.
Then I will place my Spirit in you, and you will live, and I will place you in your own land, and you will know that I, the LORD, have spoken and I have done it," declares the LORD.

Putting the paper back in his pocket, Henry thanked everyone for their attendance, again, and then sat down.

The seven men who stood as statues brought the rifles to their shoulders, took aim, and fired a volley of blanks in unison, which ruptured the previously calm sky.

Claudia jumped in her seat; Mark put a calming hand on her arm.

The seven men each chambered another round, took aim, and fired another volley. And then they did so again, one final time, bringing the three-volley salute to an end.

As the echo from the gunshots vanished over the rolling hills and the smoke drifted toward Heaven, a man in uniform raised a bugle to his lips and played taps, loud and steady, each note resounding marvelously across the countryside cemetery.

***

Not far from the gathering in Saint-James, another funeral took place that morning in Normandy. It was for young Vivienne, attended only by Gerard, his son, and his granddaughter, Vivienne. They buried the girl next to her parents, in the cemetery of a small church in the town near their home. Not coincidentally, the death year on her new gravestone matched that of her father's beside her.

Gerard gazed down at the wooden coffin. He took the *denarius* from his pocket, looked it over one last time, and then dropped it into the grave. He apologized to his sister for taking her from the forest she loved, but explained that he couldn't bear to leave her there alone, cut off from the family once he died himself.

***

Seven months later, a third funeral followed. This time Gerard's, this time coronavirus. He died alone in a sanitized, isolated wing of a hospital in Caen.

Under normal circumstances, hundreds would have gathered in that little, rural church, for Gerard was a man who'd touched many lives. But the coronavirus restrictions allowed no such recognition. Instead, Vivienne, her parents, and a few pallbearers buried him quietly in the churchyard cemetery. They laid him beside his wife, two rows away from his sister and their parents.

Vivienne was devastated, crying over Gerard's casket, so unceremoniously interred.

The End

On Thursday, February 24th, 2022, Russian president Vladimir Putin ordered his military to execute a massive invasion of Ukraine, shattering the status quo of the post-Cold War era.

Acknowledgments

There are several people without whose help or influence this book would not exist, at least not in this form. To them, I'm deeply grateful. In particular:

Lieutenant Colonel F.F. (Retired), for seeing in me a passion for photojournalism and working on my behalf to find a place for me within U.S. Army Europe.

Lieutenant Colonel C.B., for sending me on all the assignments, from the fields of sunny Tuscany to the far-flung desert drop-zones of eastern Turkey.

Sergeant H.V., Staff Sergeant J.Y., Sergeant M.P., Specialist A.W., and Sergeant First Class J.S., for being some of the best company I could have asked for during my stint with the brigade. We had some good times.

Captain James Seawright, for the illustrations. Thank you for staying up late to finish them the night before a zero-dark-thirty wake-up and a subsequent month in the field.

Dr. Benjamin Braddock, for the introduction. It couldn't have been better.

All the advanced reviewers mentioned on the front cover, back cover, and first pages of the book, for taking the time to read the manuscript and offer praise.

All the early readers, for your thoughtful comments and conversations regarding the first drafts. You know who you are. Thank you.

Giorgia Greselin, for many things. Thank you for being my first reader, and thank you for always believing in me.

And finally, Lucas Menzies, for being the best damn editor any writer could hope for. I believe you'll be remembered as one of the finest editors of our time.

That said, any errors in the text are entirely my fault.

Again, thank you all.

Works Referenced

Regarding some of the history and regional particularities mentioned in the text, I'm indebted to several scholarly and journalistic works. In particular:

I relied on UNESCO's website for the Old Town of Regensburg for information about the city's history and architecture used in the second story.

For the third story, I used the Greek Genocide Resource Center's "A General Overview of the Greek Genocide." The excerpt the Greek read to the American at the tavern is from the *Black Book; the Tragedy of Pontus, 1914-1922 ... Livre Noir; la Tragédie du Pont, 1914-1922*, which can be found through many online resources, as it exists within the public domain, but the name of the author is unknown and its original publisher is unspecified.

The Air Force Magazine's article named "The Euromissile Showdown," by Correll, as well as *The Washington Post*'s "Italian Police Move Against Terrorist Hide-Outs," by Gilbert, came in handy while writing some of the conversations between Federico and Araceli in the fifth story. Additionally, I learned much about the Appian Way from the *Dictionary of Greek and Roman Geography: Via Appia* by Smith as well as Engineering Rome's article, "The Engineering Behind the Via Appia," by Orsi.

In the seventh story, the song sung by the Alpini soldiers is called "Inno degli Alpini," or, "Trentatré." It can also be referred to as "Valore Alpino." The current lyrics were written by Camillo Fabiano, likely adapted from an older song prior to the First World War. I read about the shadowy origins of the song on the Alpini's official website, in an article named "I papà del 'Trentatrè'" by Spreafico.

For information about Hohenfels and the British NCOs kept there, I read the journal of a Private Les R.A. Foskett, which I found on the website of the Pegasus Archive. In addition, I perused the articles about Hohenfels and Stalag 383 on the official website of the 49 Squadron Association.

For the same story, I read sections of *Die Grafen von Velburg und ihr verwandtschaftliches Umfeld, Genealogische Recherchen* by Schneider as well as various articles on the official city website of Velburg, Germany. I highly fictionalized much of the content regarding the Lords of Velburg. In no way is my fiction representative of the scholarly work referenced above. I took bits of truth and distorted them. If you would like to read about the real Lords of Velburg and what scholars believe happened to them, pursue the previous resources.

About the archeological excavations of WWII-era sites that have taken place in Normandy, I read several great pieces, namely: *Archaeology, D-Day, and the Battle of Normandy: 'The Longest Day,' a landscape of myth and materiality* by Carpentier, Ghesquière, Labbey, and Marcigny, and published by Routledge; *Archaeology Magazine*'s "The Legacy of the Longest Day: More than 75 years after D-Day, the Allied invasion's impact on the French landscape is still not fully understood," by Lobell; and *The New York Times*' "The Archaeology of D-Day," by Nossiter.

For the numbers of missing service members from the Second World War, as well as information about methods used in recovering the missing, I found the official website of the Defense POW/MIA Accounting Agency extremely useful.

The interactive timeline, "D-Day. How Allied Forces Overcame Disastrous Landings to Rout the Nazis," by The History Channel, was a helpful refresher for the events of D-Day.

And, finally, regarding presidential speeches, the excerpt of Roosevelt's D-Day speech read at the funeral is from the official website of the Franklin D. Roosevelt Presidential Library. The George H. W. Bush quote at the beginning of the book can be found on the official website of the U.S. Diplomatic Mission to Germany, on the page for his speech titled "A Europe Whole and Free."